I0731395

DARK LABYRINTH

Peter David Myers

The Mentoris Project is a series of novels and biographies about the lives of great men and women who have changed history through their contributions as scientists, inventors, explorers, thinkers, and creators. The Barbera Foundation sponsors this series in the hope that, like a mentor, each book will inspire the reader to discover how she or he can make a positive contribution to society.

Contents

Foreword

First and foremost, Mentor was a person. We tend to think of the word *mentor* as a noun (a mentor) or a verb (to mentor), but there is a very human dimension embedded in the term. Mentor appears in Homer's *Odyssey* as the old friend entrusted to care for Odysseus's household and his son Telemachus during the Trojan War. When years pass and Telemachus sets out to search for his missing father, the goddess Athena assumes the form of Mentor to accompany him. The human being welcomes a human form for counsel. From its very origins, becoming a mentor is a transcendent act; it carries with it something of the holy.

The Mentoris Project sets out on an Athena-like mission: We hope the books that form this series will be an inspiration to all those who are seekers, to those of the twenty-first century who are on their own odysseys, trying to find enduring principles that will guide them to a spiritual home. The stories that comprise the series are all deeply human. These books dramatize the lives of great men and women whose stories bridge the ancient and the modern, taking many forms, just as Athena did, but always holding up a light for those living today.

Whether in novel form or traditional biography, these books plumb the individual characters of our heroes' journeys.

The power of storytelling has always been to envelop the reader in a vivid and continuous dream, and to forge a link with the subject. Our goal is for that link to guide the reader home with a new inspiration.

What is a mentor? A guide, a moral compass, an inspiration. A friend who points you toward true north. We hope that the Mentoris Project will become that friend, and it will help us all transcend our daily lives with something that can only be called holy.

—Robert J. Barbera, President, Barbera Foundation
—Ken LaZebnik, Founding Editor, The Mentoris Project

To the men and women who have the
courage to tell the truth as they see it.

And to Irv and Jeannette, who believed in
me and let me walk my own road.

Preface

The legacy of Galileo Galilei: Just what was it? His was not that he found evidence of the true nature of our cosmos, not that he advanced the technology of telescopes, but that, with the scientific method he outlined in *The Assayer*, he paved the way for all future scientific endeavors. In *Mechanics*, he gave us his observations about motion and physical mass, which consisted partly of his precursors to Newton's Laws of Motion, precursors themselves to modern physics. In short, his insistence on making observations and conclusions based on empirical evidence, not on what one author thought about the book of another author, made him the harbinger of the death of scholasticism. In so doing, he helped us shed the constraints of the Old World and effectively *pushed* us into the modern world.

Beyond that, Galileo left a legacy of courage in the pursuit of truth, and in saying and writing the truth, regardless of the consequences to one's personal security and safety. While it's true that to avoid Inquisitorial torture and rigorous imprisonment Galileo had to backpedal away from his long-held beliefs, and in the bargain had to endure his last eleven years of life under house arrest, it was too late for the Inquisition to achieve its goal of suppressing the truth; his books were being read and applied by scientists everywhere. So, in that battle for men's minds, Galileo was the ultimate victor. And that was our victory.

Courageously putting oneself in harm's way is a bar few scientists measure up to. Yet, there will always be scientist gadflies who rationally challenge the status quo by bravely poking their noses into places they don't belong and reporting on findings that threaten to set back civilization. Anyway, civilization's progress has always moved two steps forward and one step back. At times, the ratio has been worse—but regardless, we inexorably move forward. Galileo's legacy was that he successfully put his shoulder to the wheel of discovery so that civilization could move forward. Hats off to him!

The challenge to any novelist dealing with a real person is to bring their life to life. That means relying on an artistic maxim: Imagination is senior to fact. A famous filmmaker once said that art is life with the boring parts taken out. Thus, I've tried to interpolate into what we know are true events what my intuition and imagination tell me *could have* happened, could have been said, might have been done, or might have been thought. And what is art but skillful use of imagination? I hope I've used mine skillfully. You be the judge.

Prologue

It was a crystal-clear day in Florence in the spring of 1739. Long past the heady days of the High Renaissance, Florence still basked in the glories of the fruits of Florentine geniuses such as da Vinci, Michelangelo, Raphael, Titian, and Botticelli. Passing constant reminders of the output of these creative giants, Giovanni Battista Nelli, a writer, walked through the busy city streets. He was short and stocky with a to-the-manor-born appearance, although he had none of the manner so common to his class. His late father had been a well-to-do architect and had seen fit to outfit him not only with his same name, but also with a proper education. By his mid-twenties, Giovanni *fils* had become, while not as famous as Giovanni *père*, at least a budding, accomplished young man of letters, due just as much to his innate talent as to the fortune from his father's estate.

Giovanni was on the way to a monthly lunch with Dr. Lami, a family friend who was also of a literary bent. In preparation, Giovanni stopped for some mortadella at a butcher shop he had recently heard excelled at this particular sausage. As Giovanni watched, Cioci, the shop's owner, thin-sliced two generous sections of his prized mortadella and wrapped them in paper. He hoped Giovanni would become a regular customer.

Dr. Lami met Giovanni at the Inn of the Bridge, a superstructure built above the stone arches of the Ponte Vecchio that spanned the river Arno. The two of them lounged on the inn's small terrazzo and ordered antipasto and a good Chianti to go with the mortadella. The fortyish Lami was a handsome, affable man who saw his patients in the mornings and wrote poetry in the afternoons. He was a proud member of Società Letteraria del Duca, a local literary society with the coveted seal of the Grand Ducal imprimatur. Having recently sponsored Giovanni for a membership, Lami looked up inquiringly as he wrapped a slice of melon with a slice of mortadella and gorged on them. His words slurred as he chewed. "This is excellent mortadella. How are your idylls of the Tuscan countryside proceeding?" he asked.

Giovanni looked away glumly. "Slowly. I'm having a problem with inspiration. Inspiration, eh? There's something missing in my work. A certain passion."

Lami smiled complacently. "You're young, Giovanni. Don't expect to ascend from the waves of the Adriatic, perched on a clamshell like a fully formed Torquato Tasso in his prime."

Giovanni bristled at the mention of the revered poet whose works he had actually never admired. But Lami had made his point. Giovanni admitted to himself that he was reaching for instant brilliance.

Lami continued, "With patience and hard work, your good writing will come." Giovanni shrugged. "Just keep at it. If your father had lived longer, I know you would have made him proud. He wrote too, you know, in addition to his archi—"

"I know! I don't want to be my father!" Giovanni cried.

Lami quickly composed himself. "Certainly not, my boy."

He paused to think. "But I have good news for you. You can only be yourself."

Giovanni shrugged. "That's good news?"

"But you're very good at being yourself," Lami said with a smile as Giovanni laughed. "In fact, no one can compete with you on that!" Giovanni's laughter was contagious. Lami was gratified at the sudden confidence in the young man's eyes.

Satisfied that he had at least temporarily given a ray of hope to his protégé, Lami leaned back in his chair, closed his eyes, turned his face to the Tuscan sun, and cleaned his teeth with a small succession of crude toothpicks. Lami felt expansive as the warmth of the sun suffused his flesh, heating him down to his bones. He burped.

Giovanni smiled. "There's nothing like a good Tuscan mortadella."

"It's the pounded garlic," Lami replied. "Yes, we don't need Bolognese myrtle berries in *our* bologna! I also like the Portuguese version, with olives. Your new butcher should merge the Florentine with the Portuguese into a new mortadella. He'll make history." They laughed.

Lami dozed serenely, suspended in time. Giovanni was caught up in the glistening rays of the sun reflected on the softly flowing Arno, which glided invitingly underneath them and past the painted iron railing of the terrazzo—which, as the story went, had been installed to dissuade jilted, anguished lovers from rash actions.

Broken from his reverie by a muffled clatter of dishes in the kitchen, Giovanni prepared to leave and collected the mortadella wrappings on the table. As he crumpled one of them, he glanced casually at the greasy paper. *What's this?* he thought. *Handwriting?*

Giovanni read the words on the wrapper and scanned the page to the bottom. Though the writing was faded, it was clearly a letter. It was signed "G. Galilei."

Oh, Lord, he thought. *Galileo! A letter written by Galileo!* Giovanni concealed his utter excitement at the find. A letter from Galileo had been used to wrap his mortadella!

Carefully, he uncrumpled the wrapping and flattened it. Giovanni couldn't believe his luck. He looked over at Lami, who still dozed. Suddenly, a pair of young lovers laughed heartily at a nearby table. Lami jerked awake from his slumber. He looked at Giovanni, who nonchalantly folded the wrappings and stuffed them in his pocket.

"Why do you save them? Throw them out," Lami said.

Giovanni replied, "I'm going to get some more mortadella on the way home."

"I want some more too. I'll go with you."

Giovanni panicked. "No, I'm stopping at the apothecary first, and then the bank. I might be there for some time. I don't want to delay you."

"*Basta.* Another time, then."

Giovanni nodded in relief. He was keeping this find to himself.

Later, after they went their separate ways, Giovanni rushed to Cioci's. Approaching the shop, he slowed and assumed a more casual gait. As he entered, Cioci looked up from a pig's head he was trimming. "Ah, you want more, eh?" he said, chuckling. "They even come from the other side of town for it."

"No more today, *grazie,* but it was superb," Giovanni replied blandly. "I'm curious about something. I'm always shipping books to friends in Rome and Milan and I use a lot of wrapping paper. Do you have more of that paper you wrapped the mortadella with?"

Cioci smiled, his good heart showing. "*Certo, Signor.* I have a stack in the back. How much do you need?"

"I'll buy whatever you might have," Giovanni said with a nervous smile.

Cioci's eyes glistened. He thought of the profit he could make in the situation, and that he had other sources for wrapping paper anyway.

"By the way, how did you happen to come by it?" Giovanni asked offhandedly.

Cioci's mind raced. Concerned Giovanni was trying to go around him to his source, he shrugged and replied coyly, "Eh. It's my good fortune that, since last month, every few days a boy brings it to me and I give him a few scudi. Where he gets it, I don't know or care. But it makes for good wrapping, eh?"

"*Sì, sì.* It's perfect for sending books."

"*Bene, Signor,*" Cioci grinned. "Come back in a week and I'll have more for you."

Giovanni smiled back and said, "*Molto bene, e grazie.*"

But after buying what paper Cioci had left, Giovanni didn't wait to come back the following week. From then on, he sat every day, all day, in a café across the piazza from Cioci's. He waited for the boy with the wrapping paper. Day after day, the boy didn't come. Still, Giovanni sat with his wine, coffee, and panini. He worked on his pastoral idylls and glanced up frequently at the entrance to the butcher shop. He was incensed at the idea of a great man's letters becoming butcher paper. These writings were the products of the greatest European mind since da Vinci, and they were being used to wrap sausage. He wouldn't have it. Through a chance purchase, he had found his inspiration. He would preserve the legacy of Galileo Galilei.

Part One

THE WORLD OPENS

Chapter One

In June 1609, Galileo Galilei worked silently and alone in his workshop on the first floor of his house in Padua. Moonlight and a few candles illuminated the scene. Galileo bent over his workbench to grind a glass lens with the near-agonizing intensity of a perfectionist. Words came back to him from a letter he'd received from his scientist/statesman friend, Paolo Sarpi, the week prior:

My dearest friend, Galileo,

I know you will forgive me for not writing so much anymore, but the papist stilettos have left their permanent mark on my health. The pope and his minions continue to plot against me, but I will not desert the Republic by seeking refuge in England. Pray for me, my friend, that our Lord and Savior will protect me from their sharpened blades. Since your visit, which brought me so much joy, I want to tell you that the Flemish stranger has departed Venice, having found no joy with the Senate. My recommendations against his Dutch spectacle glass have been fruitful. They have refused him, and the field for these devices is left open to your efforts. I know you are embarked on producing such a device, which I'm sure will afford more power to enlarge a subject. I defer to your genius in optics and mechanics to bring your efforts to fruition.

Galileo stopped to check lens thickness measurements and to examine his grinding tool. Just the other day, he had made the error of over-grinding a lens and was still berating himself for having to start over with fresh glass. As he approached the correct thickness for the glass, he was taking extraordinary care not to go too far with it. He looked for anything that would damage the high-quality Venetian glass. Lens grinding was not an activity for the casual enthusiast, but Galileo had the patience for it. He was proud, ambitious, tall, heavily bearded, and alternately gruff, witty, and caring with his friends. At forty-six, in spite of his sturdy frame, he had been suffering for years from gout brought on by too much wine.

Moreover, Galileo's health had been seriously compromised by unknowingly inhaling toxic underground gases after he and several colleagues ventured into an unexplored Tuscan cavern five years earlier, such that he had been suffering severe rheumatic attacks and heart palpitations since. Also, suffering the earlier summer with a persistent fever, he had lain bedridden the following winter with various pains, sleeplessness, discharges of blood, and resultant depression. In times such as those, his thoughts wandered to his father, Vincenzo, who had died eighteen years earlier and who, Galileo judged, had done what he could for the boy, teaching him music and getting him educated as best he could with his meager finances. Nevertheless, Galileo thought to himself, *I'm forty-six and I've gotten no further than my father, so what's the use of all this struggle?*

And yet, he struggled on.

Galileo strained at his grinding and thought of a reply to Sarpi's letter:

My esteemed and gracious Paolo,

Words cannot express my thanks to you for giving me a chance at the spectacle glass. I would gladly welcome additional income from the sale of this glass to the Venetian Republic. When complete, my device should make objects appear roughly six times larger than with the naked eye. I will send further news when I've completed it.

His body plagued him, even now on this unusually cold summer night, and his wrists ached from the incessant grinding motions at the fixture. At times like this, Galileo consoled himself with his full mathematics professorship at the University of Padua. He enjoyed Padua's prestige and academic freedom. Because Padua was part of the independent Venetian Republic, he was even allowed to lecture against the faults he found in the philosophy of Aristotle, the Jesuits' sacred cow. Galileo felt secure that Padua was beyond the reach of the Jesuit oversight he had experienced as a student at Pisa University. At Padua, he was only mandated to give three lectures a week, which left him free to take in student boarders, who added roughly another thousand florins a year to his meager university salary.

I'm forty-six and I've arrived at a dead end, he thought. *I've been either a student or a teacher for most of my life, and what have I got to show for it? A measly few thousand florins a year, a mistress, three illegitimate children, and a mother from the pit of hell who gives me no peace. I'm a failure. What do I have to live for now? I've advanced the sciences not one whit. And what have I done to live up to my father's legacy? Nothing. He worked hard to give me a life better than his—a good education, mathematics, music theory, a father's love. But, God help me, it's all wasted. I need a major push forward. Something to give me wings and let me soar to new heights of fortune and fame.*

Yes, it mattered what others thought of him, but that was secondary to how he viewed himself. And the view wasn't great.

Galileo stopped again to let his ambition send his mind vaulting over his current circumstances to a life of independent happiness granted by an as yet unknown patron.

As would always happen at his low points, his dreams intruded on his self-pity. He imagined a patron who would leave him free to research, experiment, and write without obligations to teach or lecture. With new discoveries and consequently new books, Galileo knew he could attain the notoriety required to find such a patron, either in the nobility or the Church. As a Tuscan, he had set his sights on one of the Medicis—Cosimo II, grand duke of the Florentine Republic, whom he had tutored from childhood on and who had become as much of a friend as his royal position could allow.

The initiative in that direction was for another day, however. Tonight, his student boarders had finally quit their incessant questions on geometry, mechanics, and astronomy and had left him in peace in his workshop. He had just locked himself in and returned to work when a knock on the door startled him. Twinges of pain shot through his shoulders as he pulled his hands away from the grinding fixture. "What?!" he said, irritated. A moment passed. "That has to be Guiducci." The young man had to know how everything worked, especially the heavens, about which Galileo regretted that he could only offer speculation.

From outside the door, Mario Guiducci's voice rang out clearly. "*Professore* Galilei, I have a question."

"That's a surprise," Galileo responded. Their dialogue usually began thus, then ended in a mandatory discourse in which Galileo felt obligated to respond.

"Can I come in?"

"No!"

"Can I ask the question through the door?"

"Do I have a choice?" Galileo said. Guiducci laughed. "My purpose in existing is not to make you laugh, Guiducci. What's your question?"

Guiducci cleared his throat. He was hoarse from yelling through the thick oaken door of Galileo's workshop, which was right off a frequently chilly hallway. "The authorities tell us that perfect crystalline spheres surround the Earth."

"*Authorities?*" Galileo snorted derisively.

Guiducci continued, "Are the spheres filled with water . . . or air?"

"I don't know. Go see for yourself."

Guiducci knitted his brows. He wasn't sure if Galileo was joking. "I can't," he said, after pausing to think.

"Why not?"

"Because I can't just fly out there and look, you know, through the spheres."

Galileo had had enough. "That's not my problem. I'm busy. Go away," he said. As he returned to his grinding fixture on the workbench, he accidentally knocked the telescope housing to the floor, shattering it into many pieces. Galileo swore at the top of his lungs, "Another two weeks wasted!"

Guiducci was silent, thinking himself to blame for Galileo's outburst. "Forgive me, *Professore*. I'm going away now." Shoulders slouched, Guiducci plodded back down the hallway.

Galileo felt a pang of guilt. When he was in pain, he wasn't himself. He cared about his students, but seemingly less so when his body was acting up. He yelled through the door. "Mario?"

Guiducci stopped. His eyes brightened. Smiling, he hurried back to the locked door. "*Sì, Professore?*"

The door opened suddenly. Galileo looked intensely at his student. "Never be afraid to ask questions," he said.

Guiducci smiled. "*Grazie, Professore.*"

As Guiducci vanished happily down a narrow stairway, Galileo's guilt dissipated. But he knew it would return, as would Guiducci.

Galileo's arrogant, abrasive manner had at times lost him several friendships. But they weren't his true friends who knew his physical ailments occasioned his gruffness. Because they admired his brilliance, they accepted his flippant wit, though it was often pointed at them. Moreover, even when times were tough for him, which was often (having to maintain three illegitimate children, a mistress, and a nephew), his friends loved him all the more because he was always willing to help someone in need.

Galileo was tired from turning his grinding tool. He didn't look forward to refabricating his telescope housing. He suddenly yearned for the embrace of his mistress, Marina. Her massaging hands always eased the pain of his physical conditions. He thought bitterly about the gases in the Tuscan cave that had poisoned his bones and muscles. He wished he could turn back time. The conditions he suffered were intensified by his lens grinding, which stretched hour after hour. But he kept turning the wheel. He thought about Hans Lippershey in the Netherlands, who, the year before, had only managed to fabricate his "Dutch perspective glasses" as amusing, three-power, child's novelties—while immediately applying for a patent on them!

While Galileo had passed his physical prime, he was only then entering his prime years as a scientist. Telescope optics was not even a formal field. As such, the making of Dutch perspective glasses was virgin territory, thought Galileo. Lippershey had not even conceived of improving his lens optics, nor had he turned his spectacle glass to the night sky, which was exactly what Galileo intended. He was determined to know the truth of the world. First, he would fabricate a new housing and assemble his lenses into a more powerful device than the Dutchman's.

The latter will suffice if all the Dutchman needs is a magnified view of his neighbor's barn, thought Galileo. *I want to magnify the world.*

Chapter Two

Two weeks later, Galileo was nearly finished. He had worked fast, grinding and polishing his two lenses. He doubled his speed over the next week fabricating a four-foot tube to hold the one-inch-diameter lenses in a refractory arrangement. The result was a six-power telescope twice as powerful as Lippershey's.

To add icing to his cake, Galileo had finished his "spectacle glass" on the first clear night in weeks. Nervously, he attached it to the mounting interface of a rifle tripod he had borrowed from a Venetian naval officer. Bringing up a chair, Galileo pointed the device up at the night sky and looked through the eyepiece. All he could see were stars. Hundreds of them. He trembled with the realization that he had just made history. Awed and humbled, he crossed himself and thanked God for allowing him to be the first man to see what had never been seen before by any man in the history of the world. He was sure of that. And yet, there they were, a miraculous myriad of stars. Glistening, almost beckoning to whoever wanted to look. He felt he was looking at the greatest treasure in existence, greater than all the gold in the Vatican and all the silks and jewels of Samarkand.

Galileo scanned the night sky. *An endless sea of stars!* he thought.

Suddenly, he froze. He was looking at a densely packed star cluster unlike anything around it. And then he realized—it was the Milky Way, seen by the ancients but never magnified as it was now, exposed in detail and clearly much more than the mere glowing ball of light it had been for mankind's naked eyes for hundreds, even thousands, of years.

"I've done it!" he yelled. He had unmasked the Milky Way! His mind raced and swirled in cascading extrapolations he could not have completely voiced or encompassed even if asked to.

And then he realized something. *This is the major push forward I needed! The success that will overshadow all my failures! From this, everything I want will follow!* he thought. His smile spanned from one jowl to the other. He looked up at *his* stars. In that moment, he owned them.

Through his glass, the stars stretched forever. Galileo felt he was looking at the face of God. Slowly, he tamed his mind into rationality. *My God! How far does this labyrinth stretch? And how can we say we are alone and in the center of all this when it appears we lie only on the fringe of it?* he thought.

He immediately realized he could never ask these questions publicly, not if he valued his position at the university, or his freedom—or even his life. Being in Padua (part of the Venetian Republic), Galileo was protected from the Roman Inquisition. But once he announced his discovery, the news would travel fast—and the moment he ventured outside Venetian territory, he could be snatched up by agents of the Supreme Sacred Congregation for the Roman and Universal Inquisition, leaving him at the mercy of the Cardinals General.

Galileo didn't let such dark thoughts spoil this victory. He felt as if the entire universe had in one brief, wondrous moment opened itself completely to him. *Has anyone ever seen this?* he thought. But he had never read or heard of any such thing. What he looked at was mind-numbing, humbling, and ultimately a cause for elation. He had broken through the walls of an ancient mystery, and he knew it.

The words of Lucretius, written over sixteen hundred years earlier, came to Galileo. He intoned the words from memory:

Take the first pure and undimmed luster of the sky and all it enshrines. The stars that roam across its surface, the moon, and the surpassing splendor of the sunlight. If all the sights were now displayed to mortal view for the first time by swift unforeseen revelation, what miracle could be recounted greater than this? What would men after such a revelation conceive as impossible? Nothing, surely.

Then it was as if that open door had closed upon him forever. What he had to say was just such a revelation. A revolutionary one. Who would listen to him? He chuckled bitterly, "Only the Holy Office. And they will listen only to condemn, as they did with Bruno."

He thought of Giordano Bruno, whom the Holy Office had burned at the stake for heresy only nine years earlier. Galileo suddenly felt very lonely, like the sounds of a lute he had heard on a deserted unlit street in Padua. The hopelessness that no one would take him seriously settled on his shoulders like a sack of wet flour. He felt completely alone on Earth as he looked back up at the stars, which were slowly fading with the coming dawn.

"They'll be back again tonight," he said aloud, putting away his equipment. A firm resolve grew in him, bolstered by his self-confident ambition that he had stupidly allowed fear to destabilize. He would make the world see and understand what he saw. Nothing could stop him.

22

Chapter Three

That night, Galileo dreamed he was floating in space. Bishops and cardinals serenely floated past him on their way to Heaven. They turned to look at him as they passed, then shook their heads sympathetically, informing him he would not be allowed inside.

"Please," he pleaded. "I want to know. I want to find out."

A cardinal came abreast of him, his cassock undulating around his frail body. His eyes glared at Galileo as he said, "It is not for you to know, my friend."

After blessing him with a cross gesture, the cardinal drifted on by. Galileo heard a child's cry and awoke in a worn-out haze, recalling that he had ridden a ferry to Venice and dragged himself wearily to the house of his mistress, Marina, where he had collapsed on her bed and gone to sleep. But now their first-born, three-year-old Vincenzo, was hungry. Where was Marina? He called to her.

"*Sì, sì, Amore!*" Marina answered from another room. She had gotten out of bed, picked up Vincenzo, and had taken him to the kitchen. Galileo's daughters, nine-year-old Virginia and eight-year-old Livia, realized he was awake and screamed and giggled as they invaded the bedroom. They jumped on the bed to play with him. A tickle fight ensued, accompanied by even louder screams—after which, Galileo sent them packing. He thought about his children, whom he loved dearly. Being illegitimate, what kind of futures would they have? He mused with the idea of giving his daughters to a convent when they were older.

Galileo would have liked to spend more time with all of them, but he had his work to do. He thought about Marina, whose face, kisses, and caresses were embedded deeply in his heart. And he thought about his priest, who considered Galileo a faithful Catholic regardless of his maintaining a mistress. There were many men in Italy who had such liaisons. Thankfully, in day-to-day life, the Church seemed to look the other way about it. Regardless, thought Galileo, living in separate houses was for the best. He didn't want to rub anything in his priest's nose, especially because, per his mother's edict, he could never make his mistress his wife. Indeed, he might never marry anyone. His working hours were too irregular and weren't conducive to raising a family. Nor would he put family over his research.

Galileo considered his situation. He was largely indifferent to teaching, although he made as much money from the private students who lived in his house as he did at the university. As it was, the administration only required of him three lectures a week. He was already publishing his scientific findings on his own and needed no goading on that score.

As he lay in bed, Galileo's mind returned to what he had witnessed the night before. *I'm going to find out as much as I can, then I'll decide who to tell,* he thought. Johannes Kepler came to mind, Europe's most famous astronomer who had just published his groundbreaking *Astronomia nova. I'll finish reading Kepler's book and tell him what I've seen! Of course, he'll want one of my spectacle glasses to see for himself. I'll make one for him!*

In his enthusiasm, Galileo had forgotten Kepler had weak eyes from a childhood bout of smallpox. But Kepler would likely engage an assistant to view the stars through Galileo's glass.

His thoughts flooded in once more. Galileo was prescient enough to realize that his greatest discoveries lay ahead. To preempt any competitors, he would scan the skies rapidly and publish just as fast. With overweening hubris, Galileo exulted that once he published his discovery, Kepler's preeminence in European astronomy would be replaced by his own. Galileo's excitement grew with every passing moment. He felt this was just the beginning of a new life and a new career.

"I will be known not just as a mathematician, but as a philosopher," he mused.

He knew this was a much more prestigious appellation. "Philosopher" was a title ascribed to the scholar/scientists of the natural world; a "mathematician" was a mere manipulator of numbers.

Some weeks later, Galileo made a spectacle glass for Kepler and sent him a note with it:

My esteemed Lord,

I trust this letter finds you well. I have constructed an improvement to Lippershey's Dutch spectacle glass invention, a copy of which found its way to Venice. A mere child's toy, it inspired me to reconstitute it as a serious scientific instrument. I have greatly augmented its power to magnify the world, something Lippershey never conceived of.

Within a few weeks, Galileo received an enthusiastic reply from Kepler:

My good friend Galileo,

I appreciate the Galilean spectacle glass you've sent (note my new designation), but allowing for my poor eyesight that plagues me especially in regards to your gift, I have most regretfully been forced to set one of my students to viewing through it the wonders of the world you have discovered. Bernhard has reported back to me, astounded beyond all description at the overwhelming extent of the sea of stars that surround us. Indeed, he gushes that with this creation you have made a most certain and important contribution to science. Herr Galileo, all of us here at Prague look forward to your future discoveries.

I remain your willing and humble servant in the cause of science,

Johannes

Chapter Four

By that time, with constant lens improvements, Galileo had created an eight-power spectacle glass. Word of his invention had already spread both in Padua and Venice. Who was this celebrity scientist of Veneto? Even the doge, Leonardo Donato, the ruler of Venice, wanted to meet him. Thus, in the early morning light of a day in August, Galileo took a ferry from the Port of Marghera across the Laguna Veneta toward the docks on the northwestern end of the Isle of Venice. Galileo had taken Kepler's letter with him in case of need, as a sort of scientific confirmation of the import of his telescope. He reread it several times to himself as the ferry glided across the water. The summer air was just brisk enough to be bracing. Hunched against the breeze in his long coat, Galileo held tightly to the long maple wood case that housed his creation. He was amused by the tableau at the stern. Gulls followed the vessel, competing for tidbits thrown by the passengers. And until reprimanded by his mother, a son happily threw sardines into the air and grinned as the gulls snatched them in their beaks.

Galileo's excitement built as the ferry made its way toward the Venetian dockyards. The bell tower of the Basilica San Marco loomed in the distance. Finally, he disembarked and walked excitedly to the Piazza San Marco, where he breakfasted lightly at a café. Hoping for success with the doge, Galileo stared across the plaza at the basilica. Its beige façade gleamed in the morning light and its five spires inspired onlookers to imagine their ascent to Heaven. Capped by the golden lion of Venice and the imposing statue of Saint Mark, the central dome symbolized for Galileo the great power of the doge, who, due to local gossip about Galileo's novelty, had recently made it known that he wished to take in a view of his domain through the eyepiece of Galileo's spectacle glass. Donato had given over the details of the manner of viewing to his staff. It was decided that Galileo would meet him and his entourage in the eastern apse of the Basilica San Marco, whereupon they would proceed up to the terrazzo of the bell tower for a view of his domain from an appropriately imposing height.

When Galileo was done eating, he crossed the piazza past bustling workmen, ambling nobility, and calmly sauntering priests. He entered the edifice, crossed himself in the central aisle, and humbly took a seat, just as the daily mass began. Once the basilica's head priest had concluded his Latin discourse, two choirs would be employed that day in the performance of a mass by Giovanni Gabrieli, the doge's favorite composer. Galileo was almost late and was nervous about it. In the front row of the nave reserved for dignitaries, a tonsured priest pointed out Galileo to the irascible-looking, seventyish Leonardo Donato. He wore the ceremonial pointed golden cap and white ermine coat. Donato turned around to see Galileo, and their eyes met. The doge nodded interestedly to him. Galileo nodded back, bowing his head respectfully.

Donato was a semi-handsome man with a forceful demeanor, not unlike Galileo. The doge wondered at this genius from the mainland. Galileo looked interesting, but a bit young to be a full professor. What was Galileo like and what was this meeting all about? An adviser had intimated to Donato that Galileo's invention would ensure the security of the Republic, an impressive prospect. But the doge wondered about the advice he'd been given. Was the idea of magnifying things far beyond the Dutchman's accomplishments merely an idle fancy concocted by Galileo to gain favor and wealth from the Republic? Not likely, as the adviser who had given him word of it was not given to chimeras.

At any rate, even Sarpi has highly recommended him, so we shall see for ourselves what Galilei can do for us, Donato thought.

The priest had finished. The double choirs began their sonorous a cappella tones. Galileo felt his heart could burst from the intense purity and serenity of their voices. Suddenly, he worried what people would think if he told them he felt he had touched God when he looked through the glass. Was it heresy?

And then the voices lifted him up again as they rose and fell and rose again to ever greater heights, until his body felt very light, as if he could rise with their voices, past the winged angels' pendentives and out the dome windows, beyond the confines of San Marco and into the sky. Galileo was immensely elevated. He had never been more tied to his Holy Mother Church or more tearfully grateful and respectful of it than he was at this moment.

He prayed to God again, earnestly, that the day would be a success for him. It would surely lead to more money, which he could use, and it would bring him more renown than he enjoyed as a professor of mathematics. The future beckoned to Galileo and he strode toward it with open arms.

Chapter Five

After the mass, and before a tower bell could assault their eardrums by chiming the ninth hour of the morning, they all repaired to San Marco's campanile, better known as the "master of the house," as Venetians had nicknamed the basilica's tower. There, Galileo followed the doge and his retinue up the endless circular stairway—the doge carried by attendants in a sedan chair. Galileo followed, huffing and puffing. In spite of his aches and pains, he was hardily built and in sufficient shape for the climb.

Out of breath nonetheless, he stopped periodically, as did many others in the doge's retinue. Slowly, they made their way toward the tower's terrazzo high above Venice. Meanwhile, the doge had reached it and rested comfortably in a viewing chair just below the deafening bells, which were temporarily quiet. When Galileo emerged onto the terrazzo, all eyes turned toward him. A tripod had been provided to mount his spectacle glass. He bantered with the doge as he fixed it into place. The doge looked at him with uncharacteristically kind and expectant eyes.

After stabilizing his scope on the tripod, Galileo scanned the strip of the Lido sandbar east toward the Adriatic, looking for approaching vessels. Beyond small fishing boats in the near distance, he finally spotted a two-hundred-foot galliot making a broad reach about twenty-five miles away. Galileo turned from the eyepiece and said to the doge, "This will do—a galliot, undoubtedly captured from Barbary pirates, is making its way with a Venetian crew to the navy docks at the Arsenal. It has about thirty oars to a side."

"A galliot? I see no such vessel," Donato said.

"Of course not, Father," Galileo said. "You can't see it with your unaided eye. It's twenty-five miles away. But it will likely come within view of the naked eye within the next two hours."

"No one can see twenty-five miles out from here," Donato protested.

Galileo stood up from his viewing chair and beckoned to the doge. "Your Lordship, if you will but view through the eyepiece, I will show you."

Donato looked at him for a few moments and then got out of his chair. "Why not?" he said, moving to the viewing chair and putting his eye to the glass. "I have nothing to lose, do I?"

"Be careful not to move the device, Your Lordship, as it's precisely focused on that ship," Galileo warned.

Suddenly, the doge's eyes widened in surprise. "Holy mother of God and all the saints! I see it!" He took his eye away from the scope and looked out to sea again. "But it's not there!"

"Not yet, Your Lordship."

The doge moved his eye back to the scope. "But it's in this glass!"

"The test is whether it becomes visible in two hours, Your Lordship."

So, they waited. The doge sent for food, wine, musicians, and poets to entertain them while he pursued the business of the day with his advisers. Galileo kept his scope trained on the galliot while several in the doge's retinue checked the horizon for any sign of the ship. Finally, roughly two hours later, after much consumed wine and many recited poems, a member of the retinue suddenly shouted, "There it is! The galliot! I see it!"

Another added, "It's making for the southern end of the Lido! About thirty oars to a side, just as you described it, Signor Galileo!"

The doge stood from his chair and looked out to sea. "God be praised," he gushed. He looked at the telescope and then at Galileo, who looked quite pleased with himself. "*Professore Galilei*, you have made a wondrous thing with this device. The military ramifications are profound. If our naval officers can see ships on the water two hours before anyone else, what an advantage they would have over enemy vessels!"

"Exactly, Your Lordship. With this creation, I wish to further reinforce the naval power of Venice long into the future," Galileo said.

Everyone in the retinue stared back and forth between Galileo, his telescope, and the doge in an awed silence. They waited for the doge's reaction to such a bold goal. The doge looked at Galileo as if gauging his genuineness, then he clapped his hands loudly. "*Bravo! Bravo!*" he cheered. "*Molto magnifico, professore!* You are among the great scientists who help us see and understand the wonders of God's creations."

Galileo thought smugly to himself, *The doge doesn't know how right he is.*

Everyone else on the terrazzo followed the doge's lead and clapped enthusiastically. Then a cheer went up that could be heard far below in the piazza, causing passersby to curiously stare up at the tower.

The priest looked at the telescope and crossed himself.

"Blessed are God's works!" he said. More wine was poured. Most of the retinue stood around the telescope and took turns viewing points of interest in Venice and the surrounding islands. Toasts to Galileo were grandly and earnestly intoned.

But the praise had only just begun. Already recognized at mass with his spectacle case, a small crowd surprised him as he left the tower. Surrounding him excitedly, they coaxed, coddled, and toadied up to him for a look through his glass. It had already gotten a nickname. Who was Galileo Galilei? Only a man who invented the glass! But the glass! The glass was everything! Two hours later, Galileo bid his farewells, escaped the crowd, and was laughing and scurrying back to the ferry before another crowd could form.

Full of praise and good food, he traveled home more drunk with happiness than with wine. He was the hero of the day and his future was bright. But his real ambition—to be the hero of the age—sobered him quickly as he returned to the mainland. With what he had seen through his glass, he felt he was a witness to history in the making. A world no one had known about had opened up to him and him alone. And he was about to share it with others. As he returned to Padua, a steely gleam arose in his eyes. His immediate prize, with all its ramifications, was already in sight. It was today, more than ever before, that he saw himself as a man for the future. For kings and princes and, indeed, everyone. He stood proudly, looking out to sea as if waiting for the new world to come into view, which he knew would be built upon the logical formulations of free-thinking men.

Chapter Six

In those days, it seemed to Galileo that every momentous occasion was preceded by a gondola trip from Padua to Venice. Here he was again, gliding down the Grand Canal, headed for a party in his honor, celebrating the reveal of his perspicullum, as he called it, to the doge. The small craft dropped him off at the narrow terrace of Palazzo Foscarini, one of the most impressive buildings in the city, and the current domain of the Marchese of Castelli-Franchetti. In common with other palaces, Ca' Foscarini's principal and most decorated entrance facade faced the Grand Canal, the city's main thoroughfare. As Galileo's sense of balance adjusted to the fact that he was no longer moving on the water, he looked up at the portal. It held a bas-relief bronze plaquette by Donatello showing the sixty-fifth doge of Venice, Francesco Foscarini, kneeling in prayer to Saint Mark.

Unfortunately for Foscarini, a succession of tragedies had befallen the family estate in the mid-fifteenth century. Foscarini's only son, Jacopo—by his second wife, Marina—had been exiled for bribery and corruption by the Council of Ten. When Jacopo died, imprisoned on Crete, it had broken his father's heart. Foscarini had no interest in living, let alone in fulfilling his duties as the doge. Thus, the same council that had elected him then forced him to abdicate. Tragically, but not surprisingly, Foscarini died a week later. Still, as if in a proud rebuff to the winds of fate, his magnificent palazzo continued to command a superior position at the greatest bend in the Grand Canal, next to the Rialto Bridge.

While enduring her long bereavement, Foscarini's widow, Marina, had listened to the wrong advisers. They stood by stupidly while she mismanaged her husband's estate to such an extent that she was forced to sell the edifice to the Castelli-Franchettis. The merger of these dually long and fecund family lines had culminated in Giovanni, the eldest son and heir. And at the tender age of eighteen, he had inherited the title Marchese of Castelli-Franchetti, with all attendant lands, chattels, and rights, including the family's five prized grand estates in Veneto and Tuscany. And like hazelnut icing on a panettone, Giovanni enjoyed the status of marchese in the powerful Medici court of Cosimo II, Grand Duke of Tuscany.

At the time of Galileo's triumph in Venice, Giovanni was twenty-six, unmarried, and the preeminent target of the eligible young women of Venetian nobility. It was Giovanni—immensely rich, titled, and an admirer of "philosophers," as scientists were called—who hosted that special evening. Having recently learned of Galileo's spectacle glass through his connections at the doge's palace, Giovanni's interest in the natural world was heightened. Vanni, as his friends called him, wished to honor Galileo. In so doing, he had spared no expense.

Tall, starkly handsome with chiseled features, elegant in his bearing, and of kind and engaging demeanor, Marchese Giovanni was arguably the best catch in Venice for a girl of willing heart and requisite noble background. Invited to all the best balls and ceremonies, Giovanni attended very few of them, such that the rare sighting of the marchese only heightened young women's attraction to him. The public knowledge of his past tragic love affair only further inflamed the hearts of the palazzo maidens of the Grand Canal.

As the aging matrons of the city told it, when Giovanni was eighteen, he had fallen in love with Justine Milstein, daughter of a British coal baron (not at all Venetian, and from a Jewish family, no less—Justine was completely unacceptable to the Castelli-Franchetti). Mindful of their precarious position in Venetian social circles, Justine's mother, Rachel, took great pains to thwart the rakishly handsome young nobleman from corrupting her daughter. Regardless, the two lovers took to meeting in secret via letters exchanged through confederates. And when the confederates were compromised, the star-crossed pair took to signaling assignations to one another through secret nods and gestures. Had it not been for the alert attentions of spies in both households, the two would have been married by a rogue priest right under their families' noses.

Finally, having grown desperate and rebellious, Giovanni and Justine began to flout their affair in scandalous cohabitation ensconced in the marchese's luxurious apartments, complete with public displays of their love in the city's gondolas, streets, and piazzas, as well as outrageous flirtations in the best social gatherings. The couple's insolent behavior, often in full view of the horrified faces of the Castelli-Franchetti, was not the scandal of the season. It was the scandal of the century—at least, in the minds of the high-society gossips of the day.

Nothing could dissuade Giovanni from his romance—not long talks with his parents, the remonstrations of his siblings, nor even the family lawyer's daunting threats of disownment. These feeble attempts only increased Giovanni's ardor for Justine.

At length, because Giovanni's father did not have the heart for it, a scandalized, self-righteous uncle ruthlessly intimated that his nephew would not physically survive the coming Christmas season if he did not leave off with Justine at once. Tragically, Giovanni capitulated to his uncle's threat, and although he had broken the hearts of countless heiresses who swooned from afar over his grief, Giovanni's own heart was irreparably broken. Still, the ripe young heiresses of the Grand Canal dreamed of mending it.

Oblivious to them, Giovanni walked the streets of Venice in an almost perpetual mood of somber unreality. He had been so close to Justine, but with one swift threat he had been robbed of her forever. Seeing the bright colors of the city as mere grays and blacks, when friends and acquaintances approached, Giovanni spoke with a subdued sadness that seeped into all his days and nights and was only mitigated by the frequent balls and parties he hosted at the palazzo. On those nights, surrounded by the beauty of women, the power of men, and the gustatory delights of the Italian peninsula and beyond, he came alive. After all, he had guests in the house and he felt bound not to dampen their spirits.

Galileo, of course, knew the whole story and felt great compassion for Giovanni. The tragedy of it made Galileo feel lucky to have a woman he loved and who loved him back, even though she was not his wife. He thought about this as he stepped off the gondola onto the narrow terrace leading to the portal to Giovanni's palazzo. He had rescued Marina Gamba from the misery of prostitution and was glad to have done so.

Chapter Seven

As Galileo walked through the portal to the palazzo, he strategized how he could use this evening to advance his career. After a porter took his coat, he decided he would first find someone of stature who could introduce him to the host without him seeming needy. Possibly, the host knew someone in the Senate who could recommend his telescope. Galileo knew Giovanni to be very well connected both at the Senate and in the Florentine court of the Medici. After all, Galileo had been languishing without a broker to Cosimo II, the Tuscan Medici duke, since his broker to the duke had died three years earlier. It was true, Galileo had other intermediaries to the grand duke, but none were powerful enough to have any significant influence with him and were useful for gathering intelligence only. Such were the machinations that night of a man on a mission.

Satisfied that his strategy for the night had crystallized, Galileo entered the party full of Venetian glitterati. The strains of a Monteverdi madrigal caught his ear, emanating from the rear courtyard, the site of a reception before the dinner in the grand hall. Palazzo Foscari's external courtyard was the biggest such rear space of a private house, excepting only the doge's palace.

As Galileo neared the courtyard, he could hear the high, sweet singing voices of two women, full of the hope and enthusiasm of youth. He looked at the madrigal singers as he entered the courtyard and immediately wanted to walk over and awe them with his professorial charm.

Galileo looked almost gluttonously at the courtyard abuzz with swilling, nibbling, chattering guests, all too happy to see and be seen. Being petted by those present, various tame animals circulated among the guests, as Giovanni normally kept a small menagerie in the large courtyard, possibly to assuage the pain of his lost love. For that evening's affair, he had temporarily ware-housed the more unruly animals and ordered the tiles and walls to be cleaned with a mixture of river sand, soap, lye, and wood ash to remove the smell.

As Galileo roamed the gathering, he watched Asian monkeys swinging from low branches at the edges of the courtyard. A fat gentleman was feeding them grapes. One monkey dropped a small tart in the bouffant of a woman who didn't even notice. A tame lynx ambled by, chewing on a piece of meat. It rubbed Galileo's leg as it passed. Watching, an amused government functionary noted, "There's a Roman scientific society named after that animal."

"What animal is it?" Galileo asked.

"A lynx. They're discerning, with good eyesight."

"An appropriate *mascotte*," Galileo replied.

Elsewhere, Galileo noticed an expensively dressed noble-woman petting a llama with one hand and holding a drink in the other. Suddenly, a child, having wandered from the servant's quarters, ran by and jostled the woman's elbow. She spilled her drink on the llama, which promptly spat in her face and walked sedately away. The woman began to cry, but her makeup had already begun to run with llama spit. Her husband quickly wiped her face with his handkerchief and remarked, *"Mi perdoni, cara mia!* They spit when angered. I should have warned you."

Chapter Eight

Galileo was familiar with many of the guests. They seemed to him an exclusive club into which he might possibly be invited. He had been literally and figuratively on the fringe of them, yet here he was invited into their midst at last. His eyes flitted from one conversing group to another. Who could he ask to introduce him to Castelli-Franchetti? Who would fit the bill? Who among them might aspire to be almost an equal in status, if not in wealth, to the host?

Who else but Paolo Sarpi? He had miraculously appeared, smiling and munching the last of some bruschetta on which he had sacrilegiously spread imported brie. Holding a goblet of wine, Sarpi released from his clutch a timid, diminutive principessa with gorgeous eyes. She demurely stood back as Sarpi yelled Galileo's name, arms held out to embrace his good friend.

"Ah, Sarpi!" Galileo gasped, supremely happy to see him. He instantly realized this was the man for the occasion: as the official theologian and adviser to the Venetian Republic, Sarpi had the elegant appearance of a patrician, if not the wealth of one, and was sophisticated and astute enough to manipulate even the most recalcitrant and established members of high society.

As such, Sarpi was a welcomed fish in many ponds. Always

the consummate diplomat, steadfastly dedicated to his various missions, he circulated with equal comfort in high society and in prestigious government circles. He easily overcame opponents with his charming insouciance, bestowing his flattery on everyone and imposing threats to no one. Naturally, people wanted to do things for him. After all, as a lawyer, historian, and church figure, Sarpi had on numerous occasions proven himself to be a loyal defender of the Venetian Republic. Notably, Sarpi aided Venice with the ill-fated Venetian Interdict of 1606, securing Venice's independence from Rome's attempted hegemony over Europe.

Owing to Sarpi's incisive polemics and negotiating skills, Venice remained inoculated from the coarser abuses of the Roman Church so that even the pope's excommunication of the entire Republic had not substantially altered Venetian life. Especially due in part to Sarpi's strategies, the steadfast Jesuits, fearful of papal retribution if they stayed, had promptly decamped from Venetian territory upon news of the interdict. No love was lost in their absence. The rank and file prelates, or clergy, continued with impunity to happily perform all their usual rites and ceremonies, in effect thumbing their Venetian noses at the Holy See.

A prelate of the Church himself, Sarpi stood by and cheered them on. He saw Venice as a sort of bastion of "Reformation on the Adriatic," as he coined it. The light of independence and Athenian-style wisdom symbolically emanating from the Campanile had become a harbinger of a bright secular light dawning on Europe in the new century. This was a light for which Rome had no dark defense, save the Inquisition—something Venice feared less because of Sarpi.

In spite of his undaunted criticism of the Church, the

upper classes of Venice respected Sarpi's zealous desire for the preservation of Venice and its institutions and accorded him a status commensurate with his accomplishments. As such, in these get-togethers on the Grand Canal, he found himself on an almost equal footing with many nobles and was an ideal candidate to help Galileo seek ducal patronage.

"Galileo! Congratulations on your perspicullar triumph!" Sarpi teased. Galileo chuckled at the newly coined word. An inveterate coiner of words, Sarpi indulged in a self-satisfied smile. They embraced heartily.

"I would have been sorely disappointed if I could not have shared this evening with you!" Galileo admitted.

Sarpi laughed—at what, no one could say. Maybe it was the joy of being alive on this citrus-scented Venetian summer night with the voices cooing to them inside the strains of the madrigal. Sarpi's enthusiasm was infectious.

He's the perfect man to introduce me to the host, thought Galileo, before happily blurting aloud, "Where's the Franciacorta wine and where's Castelli-Franchetti?"

Sarpi laughed again. "In that order of priority?"

"Absolutely!" replied Galileo.

"What say you to sharing a good franzacurta with a good Franchetti?" Sarpi said. They both laughed. Two young women nearby looked over and smiled shyly, envious that these men were having fun when they were bored out of their wits from the annoying din of plump aristocrats and government bureaucrats showing off their indulgences.

Galileo turned earnestly to his friend. "Paolo," he said, "I want you to be the one to introduce me to the marchese. I've tutored Cosimo since he was a child, but protocol forbids directly approaching the duke with a proposal."

"I see where you're going. Franchetti is obviously well connected at court, but is very cautious about their protocols."

"Only out of politeness," Galileo said. He was not put off. "He has estates all over Tuscany that bank with the Medici. Don't forget, Cosimo's only nineteen. He may not yet know that the world sways to the jingle of gold florins in heavy sacks."

Sarpi chuckled.

"The fact is," Galileo continued, "the Medici Bank needs Franchetti's money more than Franchetti needs the Medicis. And Cosimo is, above all, a Medici."

"Eh!" Sarpi said, after thinking for a moment. "They wash each other's hands. I will introduce you. But the rest is up to you."

Galileo's hopes rose. As Sarpi strode away, he turned back toward Galileo and winked at him playfully, then put a finger up as if to say "Wait." Then Sarpi gestured toward the antipasto table, strategically placed next to the wine table.

When Galileo had joined him, Sarpi intoned, "First, we must fortify ourselves for the diplomatic mission ahead."

"*Certo*," said Galileo.

Sarpi looked over the wines. "First we pick the wine, then we pick the cheese."

Galileo frowned. "No, we pick the cheese and then the wine."

"Why?"

"Well . . . that's what they do in Florence."

"We're not in Florence, *amico*."

Wondering what was going on, a few nearby guests looked at Sarpi. Galileo deferred, "All right, to keep the peace, we choose the wine and then the cheese."

"*Bene*," Sarpi said, then picked up a bottle. "I choose this."

He pulled the cork and sniffed the bottle. "A good Chianti Sangiovese."

Galileo sniffed the cork. "I concur."

Other interested guests took notice of them and sensed amusement on the horizon. One asked to sniff the cork, but Sarpi stopped him. "Please. This is serious business," he said. The guest politely backed off. "Now, the cheese. I'm looking for a good parmigiana." Sarpi surveyed an array of cheese platters.

Galileo was enjoying this. Suddenly, he put up his hands. "No, no, no! This wine begs for—no, positively demands—aged sheep."

"There's no room on this table for an old sheep!" Sarpi said with a frown.

Guests laughed around them. Others drew near. A small crowd formed. Galileo folded his arms and said, "The *cheese* of aged sheep, my friend."

"Now you tell me! I was going to call the local shepherd!" The crowd laughed. "We have no shepherds in Venice. Perhaps Padua." Constant laughter bubbled around them, as well as side jokes among the guests. The waiters and butlers had stopped making their rounds with drinks and hors d'oeuvres. This show was better than the madrigals.

Suddenly, a friendly voice interrupted. "*Basta, amici!*" Heads turned toward the sound of a man's virile voice. "Gentlemen, you have my congratulations. You are the knights of wine and the barons of cheese. As to which is best—Sangiovese with sheep cheese, or Sangiovese with parmigiana—let the host decide."

"*Bravo! Bravo!*" yelled the crowd.

Sarpi's startled eyes found the source of the voice. It was the marchese! And he was addressing the two of them! Giovanni Castelli-Franchetti stood a head taller than most of the guests.

Only one man was taller than he—a well-dressed African body-guard (retained by Giovanni, as was the fad), whose previous owner in Istanbul, fearful of embarrassing revelations as to his personal life, had had the man deafened and muted. Adebe, as he was known, was well-muscled and six and a half feet tall. He lived and breathed to protect Giovanni and was always unobtrusively standing nearby.

As for Giovanni, the gleaming white teeth of his smile matched the merry twinkle in his eyes, reflecting spotty light from paper lamps hung *al Giapponese* in the courtyard.

Sarpi burst out laughing. "Leave it to the noble Castelli-Franchetti to settle things between us humble peasants!"

"*Sì, bravo! Certo, certo!*" the guests cheered. It was clear that, just as with Galileo's stress, the omnipresent shadow of sadness seemed to have already passed from his heart as he laughed with Sarpi. Guests chattered happily as they filled two glasses with Sangiovese and made small plates of sheep cheese and parmigiana for the taste test.

Everyone watched as Giovanni took a sip of Sangiovese. "Ahh, distinguished, complex," he marveled. "Vino Nobile di Montepulciano. Mmm, I can see the red tile roofs of the town with the green foothills above and the flat valley farmlands below that spread out like antipasto for the eye!"

"*Bravo, bravo! È un poeta!*" cried some guests.

Giovanni put up a finger for silence. He took a bite of parmigiano.

"How do you like it, Giovanni?" asked a guest.

A rowdier guest opined, "It's better than a sheep fart!" Everyone laughed raucously. "But what do you see, Giovanni?"

"I would tell you, but I can't in polite company," Giovanni replied. The crowd laughed and Giovanni's eyes shined merrily at Sarpi. In those brief moments, Giovanni had forgotten himself as well as the woman whose memory usually haunted him.

Giovanni put down the parmigiana. "*Superbe*," he concluded. Giovanni was always showing off his French, having "traveled the continent," as he put it.

He cleansed his palette with some water, then looked at the sheep cheese. "Now, for the pecorino," he said. After a sip of wine, he bit into the cheese, raising his eyebrows in surprise. "This is from a very healthy sheep."

Chuckles rose among the guests. Giovanni sipped his wine.

"What do you see now, Giovanni?" asked a guest.

"Well, this takes me back to when I was a child. My family was visiting our estate in Basilicata, just outside Taranto. While I played in the ruins of the temple of Poseidon one day, a sheepherder and his flock arrived. He petted his beloved animals as they quietly ate the grass among the marble columns, and then he sat and shared his bread with me. When I asked him how Taranto got its name, he told me the story of the god Taras, the son of Poseidon, who had fallen in love with the sea nymph Ariadne—"

"*Basta* with the history! Giovanni, what about the cheese?" yelled a guest.

Giovanni's rhythm had been broken. He was momentarily at a loss for words. Galileo at once recognized his discomfort and added loudly, "As he listened to the old man, a lamb came up to the sheepherder, looked into his eyes, and softly made the sound, 'Paaa-paaa, paaa-paaa . . .'"

Giovanni and the crowd broke into side-splitting laughter. Then Giovanni recovered his composure. "The years have passed, but whenever I eat pecorino, I think of that little lamb," he said.

When all the laughter and jokes finally died down, Giovanni raised his glass of Sangiovese in one hand and his piece of pecorino in the other. "As to which is the best, in honor of the old shepherd and his little lamb, I hereby declare the Sangiovese to go best with the pecorino!"

Many *bravos* were followed by the clinks of glasses. The din of the party continued.

Chapter Nine

Still laughing, Giovanni made his way through the press of guests toward Sarpi and Galileo. Reaching them, Giovanni put out his hand to shake Galileo's. "I am greatly indebted to you, Signor," he said.

Galileo smiled. "And I to you, honored sir, for this grand affair."

"Giovanni, this is your guest of honor, Galileo Galilei," Sarpi blurted.

"Ah! And as great a wit as he is an inventor," Giovanni said. "I have some news for you."

The young patrician led Galileo to a large private study on the third floor, where yet another table groaning with food and wine had been provided. Galileo reached for a quail egg and a bottle of merlot.

"This is the best merlot in Italia," Giovanni said, nodding his approval and taking the bottle from Galileo. He poured two glasses and looked at one in the light. "From the Tuscan Antinori family, who are proudly descended from Prince Antenor of Troy, the fool who allowed the Grecian horse into the city."

Chewing an egg, Galileo interrupted, "Not a popular man."

Giovanni handed a glass to Galileo. "Oh, he fled Troy, traveled up the Adriatic, and founded Venezia. But his descendants favored Toscana. My family shares cousins with them."

"And so, your news, Signor?"

"Please call me Giovanni, *comme tout le monde*."

They sipped the wine. "*Superlativo*," said Galileo.

"As is your taste in wine," Giovanni replied.

"And your news?"

"Your reputation for coming right to the point precedes you, but I'm enjoying your company too much, Signor Galilei."

"Please, call me Galileo. *C'est comme tout le monde*."

Giovanni laughed good-naturedly at this parody of him. "All right. As you know, your spectacle glass has raised much admiration in this republic. Indeed, it has been whispered to me by someone in the employ of the doge that His Lordship feels that if you were to offer your invention as a present to the Senate, such an act would not be deemed unacceptable."

Galileo was overjoyed. This was exactly what he was looking for and it had fallen in his lap. He had only just arrived at the party and he had already completed the first of his two missions. Galileo's mind spun. The doge had tremendous power over the Senate. He could almost feel the extra florins jingle in his pocket.

"I can't say this is unexpected news," Galileo said. "The doge was fascinated with the perspicullum."

"I'll wager he was. When can I look through it?" Inundated as he was with such requests from the stars in the social firmament, Galileo could not hide a slightly fatigued reaction, which Giovanni recognized. "Of course, we Venetians keep you up at night, clamoring to see Heaven's wonders."

"I need time to write and research."

"What's stopping you?"

"With what they pay me? I have to take in students to my house just to stay alive. And I lecture three times a week, which takes preparation. There's a future for me in the Medici court. I can follow my path there."

"But Cosimo is too young—"

"He's nineteen! He's a man!" Galileo instantly regretted raising his voice. He searched Giovanni's face for signs of displeasure, but there were none.

Instead, Giovanni nodded contemplatively. "I see your point. As a matter of fact, I happen to be related to Cosimo, through my great-aunt on my father's side who married a Medici relative."

Galileo raised an eyebrow. "You have cousins everywhere."

"It's very convenient."

"Regardless," said Galileo, "as much as I love Venice, I must accept what fate God offers. Given that parameter, I shall forge a path to bring knowledge to the world."

"A lofty and ambitious goal, Galileo."

"I have risen to it."

"Ah, and modestly so."

Galileo had warmed to Giovanni's teasing. "Modesty, as my friends will tell you, is not one of my faults."

"So I've heard," Giovanni said. They both laughed. The merlot was getting to their heads.

Giovanni considered him for a few moments, then said, "If I help you with Cosimo, would I be doing God's work?" Galileo smiled and nodded. "Good. I'm tired of buying indulgences!" They laughed.

"As for me, I can't afford them," Galileo added.

"You don't need them. You're a star in our Venetian heaven,"

Giovanni said, then enthusiastically shook Galileo's hand. "I neglect my guests. You'll excuse me, I'm sure."

Galileo nodded as Giovanni walked off abruptly. But the glow in Galileo's eyes reflected the success of his second mission. Another man as well acquainted with astrology as Galileo would have considered the stars aligned in his favor, but Galileo was too level-headed for that. That night, he took a ferry back to Padua and continued working on his optics.

Chapter Ten

Two months later, in October 1609, Galileo offered an improved eight-power telescope to the Venetian Senate, which heartily accepted it and invited him for a formal presentation. The evening was opulent and memorable, especially because the Senate had doubled his salary and awarded him a lifetime teaching professorship. Immediately thereafter, Galileo was hounded weekly for demonstrations of his spectacle glass, such that he began refusing any invitations that necessitated trips to Venice and the daunting Campanile steps. Now emerging from relative obscurity, Galileo enjoyed his rising celebrity status. The gentleman scientist had his sights set on—and was most certainly meant for—bigger things.

Regarding those bigger things, and notwithstanding the addition of Giovanni to his patronage network connecting to Duke Cosimo, Galileo continued to nurture his longstanding friendship with Belisario Vinta, his old teacher at the University of Padua who was recently appointed as the first secretary of state of Tuscany, reporting directly to the selfsame duke. Galileo warmly congratulated Vinta on his appointment to such an important position. He made sure to inform Vinta of his latest successes with the Venetian doge and the Senate, while mentioning casually that he missed his visits to Florence (the duke's seat of power).

The only things that humbled Galileo in those days were the magnificent sights through his telescope. At the end of November, he examined the moon and discovered it to be not a virginally pristine denizen of the sacred "celestial spheres" (so said the prevailing and heavily worshiped Aristotelian liturgy of the last two thousand years), but a pitted, pockmarked orb with mountain ranges, hills, and valleys not unlike Earth's. He knew this was another groundbreaking discovery, but he anticipated only minor protests from the entrenched Aristotelian philosophers about it. Never could he have been more wrong.

In the back of Galileo's mind, where he hid things he didn't want to confront, he knew this reality he offered threatened to disrupt centuries of calcified, regimented regurgitations of what some men thought about what other men's thoughts. Galileo was intelligent enough to know that lifetime salaries, which depended on the accurate parroting of Aristotle's and Ptolemy's sacred scriptures, could be wiped out from the onslaught of his discoveries. But those hacks who plied their outdated theories across the face of Europe would not go down without a fight.

Galileo wrote to Sarpi, at the time:

My examinations of the moon in all its phases means that the world is made up not of pure, unsullied objects populating inviolate spheres. In fact, the moon is a world not too dissimilar to our own. Thus, I have concluded that the spheres are mere fluffy confections of man's imagination. Instead, I believe the world to be comprised of imperfect globes in the dark and pitiless labyrinth of space, which is not a home to perfect spheres but a vastness beyond comprehension populated by lonely, wandering orbs. But what captivating unknown discoveries await us in that labyrinth? What are those worlds beyond our reach, but no longer beyond the reach of our eyes? Were they created by God only to illuminate the Earth? But who shall dwell in these faraway places? Are they inhabited with rational creatures like ourselves, and do they have souls to be saved? I confess to some confusion on this point, but these are not questions I can put to my local priest.

This last, Galileo knew, was grounds for excommunication, or at least a cardinal's shot across his bow—the idea of rational beings on other planets! "Outlandish heresy," a churchman would say! However, Galileo trusted his friend to keep his confidence about such thoughts. After all, Galileo wasn't of a mind to constrain himself within the rigid walls of Church dogma about man and the universe. Only to a certain extent did his faith in God keep him in line, and it did so only within social contexts, not scientific ones.

Galileo had been known for years, even as a student at Pisa University, for his incessant challenges of Aristotle's less significant theories. But now, his fascination and coldly impartial examination of the natural world, coupled with the open mind of a scientist (which he epitomized), had led to him to these discoveries. And like an ugly chrysalis breaking out from its constraints into a lovely butterfly, within him emerged a new self-perception as a natural philosopher, rather than a mere mathematician. Satisfied at having expressed some of his deepest questions, Galileo closed his letter to his friend, "In God, I trust. In my senses, I depend."

And depending on his senses, over the last few weeks of 1609, Galileo diligently observed the moon night after night, sketching what he saw in his scope and aching from the cold of the night air, which penetrated deep into his aching arthritic joints. Pushing aside all thoughts of pain, he dated each sketch. With each new view of an imperfect moon, his excitement grew exponentially about sharing another discovery with the world. *It had to be in a book*, he thought. This one warranted more extended discourse than a mere pedantic treatise to be glanced at and cast aside by the casual reader.

Chapter Eleven

The year 1610 came, and with it came another gift from God, as Galileo viewed it. On the particularly cold night of January 7, Galileo noticed something new in the heavens. He was looking at Jupiter when he saw what appeared to be three bright stars near it. Six days later, he saw a fourth star near Jupiter. With deepening excitement, he kept a nightly log of these stars until he realized they were not stars but Jupiter's heretofore undiscovered satellites!

"My God, my God, what have you given me?! You have trusted me to tell the world about the four moons of Jupiter!" Galileo shouted.

He got down on his knees and prayed he would be worthy of everything God was revealing to him. He cried for a bit, mostly about all the snubs from arrogant professors who considered him nothing but a lowly magician. Now, he felt he was being lifted up by God as His chosen one to spread this news to the world. Never in his wildest imaginings did Galileo think his dream of recognition would be fulfilled so majestically.

On the heels of this event followed Galileo's further disruptive observations of a new planet, Saturn, with shapes stretching beyond its edges that he referred to as ears. He also made definitive observations and drawings of the movements of sunspots across the surface of the sun, which, to his mind, showed that the sun was not stationery, but revolving on its axis. So much for the immutability of that sacrosanct sphere. And so, more Aristotelian delusions about yet another supposedly pristine and stationary celestial orb were consigned to oblivion by the "Paduan upstart," as those whose scholastic careers Galileo threatened were wont to call him. His academe-rattling, if not Earth-shaking, discoveries were coming fast and were arguably more groundbreaking than any in the last two thousand years. And thanks to countless salons, dinner parties, and various networking opportunities for Galileo to promulgate the theories underlying his observations, the "irreverent Paduan gadfly" could no longer be ignored by the sainted academic establishment whose very livelihoods were being threatened every time he opened his mouth in front of whatever influential audience happened to be present.

As to a forum for his ideas, Galileo had no lack of audiences. After a short break from teaching, during which he began in earnest to write about his discoveries, Galileo finally returned to his lectureship at the University of Padua. When he entered the lecture hall in the University of Medicine, he deduced that his newfound reputation must have preceded him. The hall had a capacity of one thousand and, in deference to the popularity of his talks—this was all prior to his discoveries—the university had made it available to him for as long as he liked. But today, it seemed that half the student body had turned out to welcome home the conquering hero of astronomical wonders. The place was packed to the rafters. Not only were all the seats filled, but eager students were wedged into every available crevice, their eyes glued to Galileo as soon as he walked in the door.

In recent years, he had been used to members of the nobility and other dignitaries attending his lectures. But on this day, in the front rows he recognized not only young Ferdinand II, son of the Austrian archduke and soon-to-be Holy Roman Emperor, but also the landgrave of Hesse as well as the princes of Alsace and Mantua. In the back of the hall, stewing in his own rage, sat Angelo Sobrini, a scrawny, disgruntled assistant professor who had been recently passed over for a promised full professorship due—ironically, he thought—to Galileo's "rising star." With every venerating look a nearby student gave Galileo, Sobrini's bitterness grew, until he suddenly left the hall in a huff, resolved to avenge himself for his commandeered professorship.

Given the sometimes hostile environment in which Galileo found himself, it became increasingly urgent for him to seek the protection and support of a powerful patron such as Cosimo, Grand Duke of Tuscany. He had not forgotten Giovanni Castelli-Franchetti's helpful offer, but he did not want to bypass or offend his chief patron, Belisario Vinta. Though not familially related to Cosimo, Vinta seemed to be in a much more powerful position than Giovanni to help Galileo with the duke. And yet, Giovanni's family ties were strong. Who to depend on? Galileo toyed with using the weaker of the two (Vanni) to plead his case with the more powerful one (Vinta), but he couldn't arrive at a definite course of action.

It was a happy coincidence that, the next day, Galileo received a letter from Giovanni explaining that he was planning to talk to Cosimo about Galileo's discoveries. Galileo made his decision; he wrote back urging Giovanni to contact Vinta in Florence instead. But when Giovanni got the missive, he promptly ignored it. He wasn't used to pursuing intermediaries to persons of power because he had literally grown up around those in power.

Ultimately, however, this fit hand-in-glove with Galileo's late January letter to Vinta. The new year of 1610 made Galileo feel his chance might slip by. As he wrote, he intoned a Latin proverb to himself: *Audentes fortuna juvat* ("Fortune favors the bold").

Galileo's note read:

Honorable Sir,

It is with great excitement that I tell you I am lately and continually humbled to my very knees at the history-making sights, these gifts from God, these momentous astronomical discoveries with which our Lord has graced me. The mountains and pits on the moon, visible only through my perspicullum, have now been eclipsed by yet more and greater celestial wonders.

I'm almost ready to publish my discoveries and I'm thinking about how I shall name the stars that circle Jupiter. I'm thinking of naming them the Cosmic Stars, because their discovery implies a new view of the world in which we find ourselves. Or, closer to home, I could name them Cosimo's Stars, unless you think it presumptuous to do so. I am also entertaining the name the Medicean Stars in honor of the duke's family. Might I inquire as to your preferences in the matter? You would do me a great service if you could let me know.

The result? Vinta wrote back in early February, with

uncharacteristic promptness, reflecting the importance of Galileo's discoveries:

> *Your idea of naming after His Highness the new stars you have discovered is generous and heroic and in keeping with your unique and wonderful genius. And because you have done me the honor of asking my opinion about what name to give these planets, whether Cosmic Stars, Cosimo's Stars, or the Medicean Stars, I openly state my feeling that the latter will be more appealing, insofar as the name Cosimo is shared by many, whereas the Medicean Stars would be wholly attributed by all to the glory of the royal name of the Medici Dynasty and its city-state of Florence. And so I firmly hold to the latter.*

Vinta had spoken. In one fell swoop, in his quest to join the Tuscan court, Galileo had made a teammate and veritable co-conspirator out of the duke's secretary of state. Galileo responded with thanks, indicating the stars would be so named. And, no doubt, Vinta shared the happy news with his duke, who would have been more than gratified at Galileo's grand gesture. The duke's favor had been successfully curried, so confirmed in Vinta's next letter, in which he wrote that it was time to bring Galileo to the duke's court, that the suggestion had found favor with Cosimo, and that Vinta was moving ahead to effect that happy circumstance. It appeared that Galileo's placement at court was all but a fait accompli.

Chapter Twelve

As his book neared completion, Galileo's excitement ascended to new heights. He was convinced his endeavor was a God-given mission to reveal the truth of the world: the cosmos. Fortunately, orders for his "Galileo tube" were pouring in from the more informed nobility of the day—intellectuals, scientists, and astronomers all over Europe, including England. Galileo excitedly hired more assistants to fabricate and ship his perspiculli. While some customers had problems finding what he had found in the vast night sky, many others were elated to view a Cosmos they had never even imagined, including Galileo's specific discoveries.

But the news that not every customer was able to find the moons of Saturn or Jupiter proved fertile ground for slanderous accusations about Galileo that sprang up in Europe like mushrooms after a rain. Galileo was, however, too inundated with endless adulations and was rising too fast in scientific, social, intellectual, and Catholic hierarchical circles to care. And if he had given it any thought, he would have been more stunned than angry. Stunned, because his intellect had matured in the prestigious enclave of the University of Pisa, where he had locked collegial horns with professors and students alike. As such, he had developed that peculiar naiveté found universally among gentlemen of learning that colleagues, whether or not they agreed with one another, would respect each other's divergent viewpoints out of the civility of their profession.

The current scene was starkly different. Suddenly, Galileo's revolutionary worldview threatened the salaries of European Renaissance pedants who hypocritically spouted the ideal of intellectual freedom while squelching any ideas divergent from theirs. Galileo was used to healthy debate, and he welcomed it. But he was not used to their insidious black propaganda, calculated to destroy his reputation and his livelihood. Partly because he knew propaganda from various quarters could undermine his newly established prestige, and partly because he knew his reputation might eventually be pecked to death by small-minded naysayers, Galileo speeded his progress on the book. He would definitively put the controversies to rest.

Never did he imagine the results could be otherwise. Because his discoveries threatened the foundations of sacrosanct Aristotelian and Ptolemaic worldviews, he told himself and anyone who would listen that he would not bother trying to "save the appearances of the heavenly spheres." Instead, he would obliterate those "fossilized fantasies of bygone millennia." With one stab of his piercing intellect, Galileo was ardently stripping away the mere appearances of the natural world in favor of the underlying causative truths. He was a revolutionary. He had become the first real scientist.

And true to form, even before Galileo had a chance to publish any of his theories, a minority of Jesuit priests, ever the guardians of Aristoteliana, refused to even look through the perspicullum. Instead, they began a whispering campaign about the groundlessness of his theories, inciting a period of ridicule and recriminations. Tides of antagonism swept back and forth between Galileo and various members of the Jesuit Roman stronghold, the Collegio Romano. As Galileo wrote to a friend:

These self-styled scientists are more inclined to insist on their own rightnesses than they are in finding truth. Thus we inherit from them these strange celestial spheres, these strange "scientific" truths from men who should know better but are more interested in asserting their rightness than in being right. Truth is built by those who have the breadth, balance, and, frankly, the sanity to see also where they're wrong or where they don't understand some novelty.

Chief among the Jesuit arguments at the Collegio Romano was the notion that Galileo tubes had lens defects that produced illusory points of light and images, including the spurious stars of Jupiter. They claimed that Galileo's supposed discoveries failed the key test of scientific verification: reproducibility. Galileo had nothing good to say about them when he referred to them in a letter to the astronomer Kepler: "These men fancy that philosophy is to be studied like the Aeneid or the Odyssey, and that the true understanding of nature is to be detected by the collation of mildewed texts."

Kepler, in his turn, mocked a letter he had received from Martin Horký, a great attacker of Galileo, by quoting his text, "I will never concede his four new planets to that Italian from Padua, though I die for it."

One day, a member of the Venetian Senate received a letter from Sobrini that accused Galileo of having a mistress, Marina

Gamba, who had birthed three children by him. This was by no means an unusual circumstance; however, it flew in the face of the conventional morality of the day, to which Venetians—and, more importantly, their senators—paid lip service. Fortunately for Galileo, the senators had just accepted his telescope and had doubled his salary, so the response Sobrini received from the Senate merely stated, "If Galileo has a family to provide for, he is even more in need of his professorship than we imagined." So quickly and efficiently had the Senate dispensed with Sobrini that Galileo never even heard of the accusation. Why bother Galileo, they reasoned, when he is raising the university's stature on the continent with the marvels of his astronomical discoveries?

Nevertheless, many barbs such as Sobrini's did manage to prick Galileo as he went about his writing, research, and teaching to the point where he complained in a letter to Orazio Grassi, one of his supporters in the Collegio Romano, that he wished those of narrow minds would leave him alone to work. But Grassi could do nothing. The times were not ripe for protests; the ramparts of Aristotelianism had not yet been demolished by rebels such as Galileo, nor had the Jesuit Order ever been constituted to making drastic changes in "accepted philosophic [scientific] thought" as it related to the biblical teachings the order was sworn to uphold.

Meanwhile, in spite of a few Jesuits' attempts to silence Galileo, his ideas had sprouted among other open minds at the Collegio Romano, all the way up the chain of command to Claudio Acquaviva, the superior general, who for political reasons chose to remain noncommittal, but was secretly excited at the prospect of viewing Galileo's discoveries.

And as for Christopher Clavius, a friend Galileo had made at the collegio, the senior astronomy professor was initially noncommittal about his former protege's discoveries until he could confirm them with his own Galileo-style telescope. In the meantime, he remained in an almost continual state of annoyance due to incessant requests from teachers, students, and lay Catholics and high churchmen for confirmation of Galileo's new stars.

Frustrated by the lack of Galileo's perspicullum, Clavius could do nothing but write an impatient letter to his old friend:

It's well and good that you're writing your book, Galileo. But as scientific and scholarly as it will probably be, if your book is anything like your earlier writings, it will not be enough to silence the yelping hyenas. If you must, to stop all the rumors flying about, send me one of your double eyeglass devices so that I may confirm the heavenly phenomena you have observed. Believe me when I say that I do not exaggerate: I am harassed daily for an opinion on your astronomical claims. If only to save my sanity, and not the appearances!—I jest—please send me your "Galileo tube" without delay.

Recognizing the value of having Clavius on his side in the fast-growing controversy, Galileo wrote back:

Honored Signor,

I'm gratified about and very appreciative of our correspondence. Further, I welcome the addition of your conclusions to my own in my forthcoming book, and I am expediting the fabrication of a double eyeglass especially for your use. It will be sent to you as soon as it is ready.

As always, with great affection, I am your loyal servant,

Galileo

To "your loyal servant," Galileo should have added "and consummate courtier."

Chapter Thirteen

During that period, Galileo was invited to forums at the collegio to discuss his theories with a small minority of Jesuit naysayers who were determined to put an end to his revolutionary intrusions on their theoretical constructs. However, they didn't count on Galileo's formidable debating skills, which left many of their arguments in smoking ruins. Some of them persisted in defending their outmoded theories and engaging in veiled insults and falsehoods, which eventually rebounded mercilessly. At the salons they attended in Rome, they became victims of Galileo's eloquently and ruthlessly defended observations. Much to the delight of his admirers, Galileo became known for trouncing his opponents in these salon debates. He had found amusement in such "discussions" since his student days at Pisa. But, sensing the evil intent of his adversaries in these outwardly friendly colloquies, he took no prisoners.

Grown impatient with the huffings and puffings of their illogical fellow prelates, many other Jesuits took to reading Galileo's open rebuttal letters to his naysayers as a form of amusement. The fad caught on, and one night Galileo found himself in the salon of a nobleman who admitted his eager anticipation for a hilarious show in which he expected Galileo to cut his opponents to ribbons with his ruthless logic. The nobleman was not disappointed. As an early adopter of the Galileo tube, he had been quite gratified when he'd learned that his social position in Venice had risen due to his prescient association with Galileo.

But one day not long thereafter, Galileo received a letter from Giovanni Castelli-Franchetti. (Although he'd been tutoring Ferdinando's son, Cosimo II, during the summer breaks up to 1608, he had never established a firm enough foundation to address him directly with his proposal.) "My dear friend, Galileo," wrote Giovanni, "I have been staying at Palazzo del Duca for the past few days. During this time, I've had our conversation at the party last year uppermost in my mind."

So Giovanni *was* directly accessing the duke, as Galileo had surmised. Galileo continued reading:

Last night at dinner, it was my good fortune to have cousin Cosimo all to myself for a time. To my surprise, as soon as we were alone, the grand duke asked how you were, being as how he has not seen you for two years. He told me that he still misses your instruction and inspiration, and that he found it sorely disappointing that you had left Pisa University for the University of Padua. I told him how all of Venice has been entranced by your momentous discoveries, of which he had already heard. He is in great awe of you, Galileo. So, I found that to be the exact moment to bring up that which you desire: I told him of your one disappointment in life, aside from various vexing family matters, that you have no time to research and write on your own because, to supplement your teaching income, you have been forced to take in student boarders.

Galileo, I have to tell you that when I mentioned your less than ideal circumstances, Cosimo shook his head as if he were having none of that. I quickly added that you have something in mind that could remedy the situation but that, out of respect for him and for the dignity of his title, you have held back from asking him about it. His response to me was this, and I remember his exact words: "Basta! Have him ask! I can't wait to see what he sends me." With these words, a light came over Cosimo's young face. There was the innocent, gleeful look of childlike excitement in his eyes. So, there it is, mon ami.

Galileo put down the letter and took a deep breath. Years of stress and unhappiness dissipated from his countenance. Galileo continued reading Giovanni's final words: "I leave the matter in your capable hands to dispense with, as I know you certainly will. And I remain your loyal friend always."

Giovanni had signed the letter simply, "Giovanni." Words could not have described how Galileo felt putting down Giovanni's letter. He leaned back in his chair and closed his smiling eyes, which flooded with tears. His dreams really were coming true. He opened his eyes and contemplated what to write to Cosimo. Having crystallized his thoughts, he leaned over his desk and began to write.

Some time later, Galileo paused, looked at what he had written, then threw it away and grabbed another sheet of paper. Putting aside his feelings of inferiority in social position and in his supplication to Cosimo, as well as his pride, he set his most intense thoughts to words: "To the most honored prince, your Serene Highness, Duke of Tuscany . . . Your Excellency, I trust you are well and am heartened that you have been looking forward to hearing from me, so I will get straight to the point."

Galileo continued by introducing Cosimo to the newly discovered moons of Jupiter. He wrote:

Evidently influenced by divine inspiration to serve Your Highness, it is no wonder that I, most desirous of your glory, might show how very grateful I am towards You. Hence, since under your auspices, most serene Cosimo, I discovered the stars unknown to all previous astronomers. I decided by the highest right to adorn them with the name of your family as the Medicean Stars.

Having labored for the past twenty years using the little talent God has granted me, before my life comes to its close, I wish to produce a number of written works and to have them published such that they bring credit to those who favored me in this undertaking. These works will certainly be of more help to present and future students than the small amount of my life's time that I can afford them at present. Of leisure, I have very little, as I must support my family from my public and private lectures. I spend the best hours of every day at the request of this or that man, thus my lectures and domestic pupils are a great hindrance and interruption of my studies. I wish to live entirely exempt from these obligations, and to return to my native Tuscany. If your Serene Highness were to give me leave to complete my works without the necessity of lecturing, then I could gain my bread from my writings, which I would always dedicate to my master.

These books I have to finish include one almost complete on my recent and astounding discoveries made in my observation of the heavens and what this can mean for the future of astronomy;

two books on the structure of the universe, full of philosophy, more astronomy, and geometry; three books on the first principles of a new science of motion, no one having isolated this as of yet; and, finally, three books on mechanics, as well as treatises on sound, speech, light, colors, tides, the motions of animals, and the military arts, including fortifications, assaults, surveying, artillery, and the use of my geometrical compass, which I dedicated to your Serene Highness and which has been fabricated into the thousands all over Europe.

I say nothing as to the amount of my salary, relying on the graciousness of your Highness. Finally, on the title of my service, I wish that to the name of Mathematician your Highness would add Philosopher, as I have studied a greater number of years in philosophy than the number I have in mathematics.

Based on my past, which has had its share of not mean accomplishments, I humbly predict a bright future for myself, which, however, could be brighter still were I to be settled in Tuscany and writing these books for your Serene Highness, and for all the world, to read.

Your loyal servant,

Galileo Galilei

Galileo smiled as he put down his pen. *All the more reason,* he thought, *that I must finish the book of my astronomical discoveries as soon as possible.* But the letter, at least, would be sent to Cosimo the following day.

Galileo went outside to tend to his garden. The air was

invigoratingly fresh, if a bit too breezy, but he felt guilty looking at his tomato vines, which had needed tending for the past two months. Not wanting to confront the muscle and joint pain involved in retying the vines, Galileo let his mind wander. He looked at a line of fifty-foot cypress bordering a frontage road in the distance. Whenever the Alps's finest north wind kicked up, a chorus line of cypress branches rustled their loud and crackly song in unison. In defiant solidarity, they had long since decided to brave the wind's intermittent onslaughts, just as their ancestors had done since Etruscan times. Galileo shivered, went inside, and had a student bring him a goblet of mulled wine as he reread his letter to Cosimo. Having satisfied himself with the politeness and discretion of his letter, Galileo sealed it and prepared to dine with friends.

Chapter Fourteen

Ultimately, the Medicis gratefully accepted Galileo's request to name the moons in their honor.

Meanwhile, Galileo's mind waxed creative. In a few weeks, his book was finally done and off to the publisher. He didn't even wait for advance copies to be sent to his friends for their comments. In short order, *Sidereus Nuncius* (or *Starry Messenger*) was published in Venice by the printer Baglioni on March 13, 1610. Galileo made sure copies of his book as well as his perspiculli were sent to Clavius in Rome, as well as Vinta and the grand duke in Florence. The latter two, of course, read the book immediately and requested Galileo meet them in Pisa to show them Jupiter's moons, as they were unable to find them using his glass. In the meantime, the first edition of Galileo's book immediately sold out all across Europe and England, and copies of his perspicullum sold as fast as he could make them.

In his book, Galileo had methodically sketched the mountains he'd seen on the moon, observed that tiny stars made up the Milky Way, and claimed to have seen (but not understood) the rings of Saturn, as well as the Medicean Stars orbiting Jupiter. Galileo's writings aimed to prove true the sixteenth century theory of Copernicus, which suggested that the sun was the center of the universe. In his book, Galileo claimed dispassionately that the planet Venus revealed phases such as the moon's, therefore Venus must orbit the sun, not the Earth. Galileo knew all his discoveries were compelling evidence for Copernicanism, although not proof.

Within a month and a half of the book's publication, Galileo began receiving letters from respected astronomers—such as Thomas Harriot in England, Joseph Gaultier de la Vallette and Peiresc in France, and Simon Marius in Bavaria—all wanting to see Jupiter's moons for themselves. Once he had sent them all perspiculli, they accomplished that and wrote to him in that effect. Reading the collection of their congratulatory letters one day, Galileo held them to his chest as tears fell from his face. His discoveries were real and profound. The Cosmos was much larger and more star-populated than anyone had previously supposed. His perspicullum had proved it, his book had explained it, and now other astronomers were trying to confirm what Galileo had gleaned from the heavens.

Many were not convinced, however. They claimed his spectacle glass had defective lenses that produced points of light and images that were simply not there. They maintained that there were no moons of Jupiter. The naysayers felt their argument was strengthened by the fact that only a few astronomers, using Galileo's spectacle glass, were able to visually verify discoveries.

The weeks went by. Galileo became more and more apprehensive while waiting for Clavius's reaction at the Collegio Romano. Whenever he got too worked up about the lack of a response, Galileo spent time in his garden, nurturing his beloved plants. Finally, a letter from Clavius arrived.

Nervously, Galileo opened the aging professor's missive. Clavius had included with his letter an excerpt from his own book, *Sphere*, which was nearing publication. Galileo read apprehensively as Clavius discussed his perspicullum: "This instrument shows many more stars in the firmament than can be seen without it, especially in the Pleiades—"

Galileo's eyes lit up. His friend had seen, as he had, the greater collection of stars in that constellation! Savoring the words, he read them over again and felt his heart would burst. All his work, the late-night observations on his roof in horrid winter weather, the painstaking scribbling and sketching until his fingers grew numb from the cold—all his efforts had been recognized and acknowledged by one of the opinion leaders at Europe's summit of Catholic learning!

Galileo wondered what else his old mentor could possibly say about his telescope. He read on: "And when the moon is a crescent or half full, it appears so remarkably fractured and rough that I cannot marvel enough that there is such unevenness in the lunar body." Then came a secretly hoped-for blessing from on high, but in a form beyond Galileo's wildest imaginings. Clavius ended his book excerpt with this: "Consult the reliable little book by Galileo Galilei, printed at Venice in 1610 and called *Sidereus Nuncius*, which describes various observations of the stars first made by him."

"First made by me!" exulted Galileo. "First made by me!"

But Galileo's joy was shortly blunted. Simon Marius, the Bavarian astronomer who initially confirmed Galileo's discoveries, had since published his own book in which he claimed prior discovery of the "stars" orbiting Jupiter. Galileo filed formal protests with whichever authorities he could alert. At the same time, he trained his logical mind on Marius and found that, not being Catholic, Marius was still operating on the Julian calendar, rather than the Gregorian. Thus, when the ten-day difference between the two calendars was reconciled, it was determined that Galileo had notated his discoveries about Jupiter one day earlier than Marius! Galileo had saved his own priority of discovery.

Predictably, overall, Galileo's book poured gunpowder on a log fire. No one in the intellectual society of the day was ready for the sensation the book caused. Galileo was accused, and rightly so, of throwing established astronomy of the prior two millennia into a tailspin. Galileo knew that while his book contained evidence for Copernicanism, it provided no incontrovertible proof of it. His more jealous colleagues accused him in polemical treatises and at dinner parties, salons, and lecture halls of trying to pass himself off solemnly as an ambassador from Heaven. They incorrectly claimed the title of his book to be *The Starry Messenger*, when Galileo meant it to be *The Starry Message*.

At bottom, the self-styled scientist-clerics, those high priests of science were irked that a simple instrument enabled anyone to see the heavens better than they could with their naked eyes and all their years of study. They bitterly imagined that Galileo sat back and laughed at them. The greatest philosophers of the day (themselves, of course) were in danger of being dethroned by a rude slap in the face: the horrible reality that they had been worshiping Aristotle's fantasies! Some philosophers rushed to save the appearances of their other deity, Ptolemy. These men were the same scientific elite who had, almost two millennia earlier, held that the Earth rested on the shoulders of Atlas, who stood on the back of a giant tortoise, which itself rested on a bed of mud. Meanwhile, Galileo's friends became tired of hearing him say, "Why save the appearances when I have obliterated the delusions?"

By April 1611, the general public's avalanches of praise continued to pour into Galileo's house in Padua. And much to the dismay of Galileo's opponents, the Collegio Romano—by then having been urged to do so by none other than Cardinal Bellarmine, known as the Hammer of Heretics—was finally able to certify every one of Galileo's discoveries as verifiable, original, and of his own doing. Indeed, the majority of the collegio considered Galileo's discoveries monumental.

Father Clavius and Superior General Acquaviva in the Collegio Romano watched all this hubbub with some amusement. As they sat one day in Acquaviva's study, they speculated about the future of astronomy and the true nature of the cosmos, as well as Galileo's place in it.

Clavius summed it up best. "Father Superior General," he said, "until Judgment Day, there will always be a malicious few who pervert, dissemble, obscure, and evade the truth."

"Despite their brayings," Acquaviva added, "I remain concerned about our Mother Church. Martin Luther began as an inconvenience for us. Now, the Holy See considers Luther and his movement a major threat. I personally know Galileo to be a loyal Catholic, but I shudder at the thought that his adherents might someday ally themselves with the Protestants and cause a further rift with us. As for the naysayers, my main concern is that they have the facility to deceive those around them into believing their views are held by the majority."

They sighed in unison and sipped their wine. "Then, with Galileo, what are we left with as an explanation for the Cosmos?" Clavius asked. "More chaos? A less than godly organization for the stars? Or do we modify Ptolemy's theories and say that Venus and Mercury alone go around the sun, while everything else revolves around Earth?"

Acquaviva raised an eyebrow. "Preposterous. Do you expect astronomers to swallow that drivel?"

"They won't, but I know many philosophers who already have, as it saves the appearances."

"Damn the appearances!" Acquaviva sighed again.

"Then what shall we do with Galileo?" Clavius asked.

"The wine in the jug has been spilled and cannot be put back. Rather than be pilloried in Padua, he should be feted in triumph. In Rome."

Clavius smiled. "And damn the naysayers!"

Chapter Fifteen

But Galileo's triumph in the scientific world had other costs. His book had described his discovery of sunspots, and thus Galileo ran afoul of an arrogant German priest in Bavaria, one Christoph Scheiner, who made much noise about his own prior discovery of the sunspots. But, in fact, someone else had first published the discovery, though they had neglected to sufficiently observe the sunspots to determine the rotation of the sun on its axis—a critical element, because it tended to undermine the celestial spheres theory of stars and planets fixed in place.

As for Galileo, newly sheltered (almost) as he was by a formidable patron, he could afford to ignore Scheiner's protests and spoutings without even the courtesy of a reply—thus making a long-term enemy of the man. The situation was rubbed in Scheiner's nose one day when, hoping to find his own book in a prominent position on the shelves, he ventured into a local bookstore in Bavaria only to find a special display of Galileo's book at the front while his own was on an obscure shelf in the back. He stormed out angrily, swearing revenge.

Meanwhile, Galileo delayed meeting Cosimo and Vinta in Pisa as long as he could because he was putting out fires at the University of Padua. The university's leaders were furious at him as rumors circulated that he was courting the duke of Tuscany and contemplating moving to his court in Florence. Padua had already doubled his salary for life and this was how he showed his gratitude? It didn't help that other Paduan professors were protesting to their higher-ups concerning Galileo's accession to full professor with a rich salary at their own expense.

Not to be undone so easily by the mere international fame of Galileo, these professors spouted their disagreements even louder when Galileo's book began circulating to great acclaim. One of these protestors, Giacomo Brutius, made a good living teaching the orthodox dogma of the cosmos to the sons of the nobility. Feeling threatened by Galileo's discoveries and knowing of the astronomer Kepler's high regard for Galileo, Brutius resorted to outright slander of Galileo in a letter to Kepler:

Galileo tells me he has written to you and has your book, a fact that he has generally denied. I abused him for praising you with too many qualifications. I know it to be a fact that, both in his lectures and elsewhere, he is publishing your inventions as his own. But I have taken care, and shall continue to do so, that all this shall redound not to his credit but to yours.

"Oh, what a true and loyal friend! You are too kind, Brutius," Kepler intoned sarcastically, tearing the letter into shreds in his parlor at home in Prague. In that moment, Kepler strengthened his resolve to emphatically remain Galileo's friend and supporter in spite of any malicious fantasies launched at him. Shortly afterward, Kepler publicly confirmed Galileo's astronomical findings in a letter he published in Prague, "Conversation with the Sidereal Messenger." A few months later, the letter was reprinted in Florence, further raising Galileo's profile at the ducal court.

~

In April 1610, Galileo finally met Vinta and the duke in Pisa. On a rooftop of Cosimo's palazzo, he set up his *perspicullum* and trained it on what were fortuitously in view that night: his Medicean Stars circling Jupiter. And here was Galileo, meeting a former student of his, now twenty years of age, who was powerful enough to change Galileo's entire future with a casual patronage. The thought almost weakened his knees. Looking up at Galileo from the telescope, an entranced Cosimo could only say, "Wonderful! Astounding! You have never stopped teaching me, have you, *maestro?*" Cosimo meant the comment as praise, but Galileo was so sensitive about his inferior position compared to the duke's that he merely smiled without pleasure. He mumbled an awkward acknowledgment.

Cosimo was so overjoyed to view "his" stars that, presumably in thanks, he later presented Galileo with a gold medallion worth one thousand florins. "That was for my education, Galileo, not for my stars. For my stars, there is no way I can conceive of to properly thank you," he said.

"In that regard, I do have an idea, Your Excellence," Galileo suggested.

"Yes, I'll wager you do, and we'll go over that later." The duke laughed and put a hand on Galileo's shoulder, much as Galileo had done when he was tutoring Cosimo as a child.

Galileo smiled and nodded. Humiliated as he felt then, he was hopeful about the outcome of such a conversation.

Over dinner with Vinta and the duke, Galileo diplomatically broached the idea of sending out his Galileo tubes to the nobility of Europe under Cosimo's imprimatur. The duke agreed, and Galileo was inwardly elated. He had planted in Cosimo's mind the idea of sponsoring him. From there, it was but a short step to bringing Galileo to his court, thus formalizing Cosimo's patronage.

Knowing, however, that he would have to pay for Galileo's presence at court, Cosimo remained tight-fisted. This, in spite of Vinta's and Giovanni's urgings.

Finally, by late spring, Galileo's astronomic triumphs had been acknowledged in scientific and intellectual circles as monumental. Especially with Giovanni's contributions to the groundwork for Galileo's patronage, it thus became easier for Belisario Vinta to negotiate with the duke of Tuscany on Galileo's behalf to permanently ensconce him in the court at Florence. Indeed, when he had earlier read *Sidereus Nuncius*, Cosimo actually mentioned to Vinta that he felt indebted to Galileo for naming his stars "Medicean."

That April, Cosimo had seen his Medicean stars for himself in Pisa. In principle, there was to be no further delay, other than the long financial negotiations, which Vinta was used to. He knew it was always thus with people like Cosimo who had inherited great wealth. Not feeling confident in the means to earn it themselves, they were usually reluctant to spend it on anything but the most needful expenditures. As a consequence, Galileo stewed impatiently for the rest of the season.

Finally, in July, almost anticlimactically, Galileo was officially hired with an enormous lifetime salary (even larger than Vinta's as secretary of state). His appointment: Chief Mathematician of the University of Pisa, as well as Philosopher and Mathematician to the Grand Duke of Tuscany. He now had three salaries in as many cities—Florence, Pisa, and Padua. With these, he could pursue his research and writing full-time. As his French colleague Peiresc said, Galileo had *arrivé*.

Chapter Sixteen

Even so, it took the rest of the summer to smooth Paduan and Venetian feathers. Galileo was, in their view, abandoning his teaching there without abandoning his lifetime salary, which had only just been granted him in 1609. At first, the Venetian Senate and the University of Padua had hinted at legal action, but Galileo used careful diplomacy to bring them around to his way of thinking: his leaving for the Tuscan court was ultimately best for the advancement of science, which it was in Venice's and Padua's long-term interests to support. Having padded his university salary with a much greater amount from the duke, Galileo could afford gallantry. He forgave Padua's obligation to his lifetime salary. He could not, however, so easily erase his guilt about leaving his family behind. Knowing Marina's undesirable past allowed him to justify leaving his mistress, but it was not so easy to push his daughters' fate from his mind. He decided to bring them to Florence at the earliest opportunity.

Leaving on friendly terms, Galileo escaped toward Florence in September. By October, he was comfortably ensconced in apartments in Cosimo's opulent Palazzo Pitti. The rest of the year Galileo gave to establishing himself at court, making friends, and creating even more patronage relationships. Having arrived at the heights of Florentine court society, he was often approached by young thinkers and scientists who were themselves seeking patrons. As long as he could verify the credibility of these supplicants, he was only too happy to introduce them to his patrons.

Florence was alive with harvest marketplaces on almost every corner as Galileo's caravan of wagons made its way toward the Palazzo Pitti. Missing his garden already, he stopped at many stalls to buy fruits and vegetables. Once Galileo arrived at the ducal palace, Vinta welcomed him and they joined Cosimo for dinner that night, which seemed like the fruition of his dreams. Not only did they treat him as a peer, but at times they seemed to elevate him above themselves, treating him like a sort of science hero. Sipping a *digestivo*, Cosimo enthused, "Galileo, I'm happy to report that our embassies across Europe have all received copies of your book as well as your spectacle glass, so they may view the wonders you've discovered and have them explained in your unique wording."

Galileo laughed. "Your Highness, I've been called many things, but I fear 'unique' may be a soft word for 'long-winded.'"

"Not at all, starry messenger. I take great pleasure in reading anything of yours," Cosimo replied.

They all laughed at Galileo's new nickname. Then Vinta asked, "Do you find everything here to your liking, Galileo? Is there anything else you need?"

"More space for my assistants?" Galileo dared to ask.

Cosimo looked questioningly at Vinta. "I thought this was taken care of, Belisario."

"My apologies, Your Highness," Vinta said. "The carpenters are still renovating the apartments next to Galileo for fabrication of his spectacle glass."

Galileo smiled at this continuance of yet another income stream.

Still, the objections to Galileo's new ideas did not stop. Galileo, hoping not for sympathy but to share what was going on, continued writing to Kepler about the continuous attacks on his integrity as a scientist and an astronomer.

"Oh, my dear Kepler," he wrote, *"how I wish that we could have one hearty laugh together. Here, at Padua, is the principal professor of philosophy whom I have repeatedly and urgently requested to look at the moon and planets through my glass which he pertinaciously refuses to do. Why are you not here? What shouts of laughter we should have at these glorious follies foisted upon us by paper philosophers—the sort of men who fancy that philosophy is to be studied like the Aeneid or the Odyssey and that true knowledge of nature is to be detected by the collation of texts! Lately, I am forced to listen to the professor of philosophy at Pisa laboring before the grand Duke with logical arguments as if with magical incantations to charm the new planets out of the sky. These arrogant arbiters of astronomical truth have the gall to congratulate each other when it is perceived they have plucked my feathers. They, who have neither the instruments (such as mine) to verify, nor the talents to appreciate, seem to prefer the evidence of their books to that of their senses."*

Galileo was not the only one writing to Kepler, however. Martin Horký, a Bohemian mathematician traveling in Italy, had been rooming with and assisting the astronomer Giovanni

Magini. As such, he had had the opportunity to view the heavens through Galileo's glass when he was demonstrating it to Magini. After some quick and devious machinations, and knowing the controversial nature of Galileo's findings, Horký decided two things:

One, Horký opportunistically determined to better his own reputation by coming down on the side of Galileo's opponents. Thinking Kepler was one of them, Horký crafted a letter to him that oddly combined praise with doubt. Speaking of Galileo's findings, he wrote, "They are wonderful. They are stupendous. Whether they are true or false, I cannot tell."

Horký's next letters to others were full of rancorous abuse of Galileo. Another note to Kepler was full of gleeful celebration of Horký's own treachery. Having just viewed Galileo's demonstration of his glass, Horký wrote to him, "Galileo's glass does wonders upon the earth, but by means of an optical illusion, it represents celestial objects falsely. Galileo has formulated a money-making scheme to take advantage of this fact."

Then he added, "I must confide to a theft I committed. I contrived to take a mold of the glass and wax without the knowledge of anyone, and when I get home I trust to make a glass even better than Galileo's." In the perverted twistings of his mind, Horký ascribed pecuniary motivations to Galileo, presumably to direct attention away from what Horký was planning. Unfortunately for Horký, his plan later backfired, and unexpectedly so.

In Italy, Horký found only a lack of vocal supporters for his attacks on Galileo. Most astronomers of the time tended to be fence-sitters, preferring not to put their careers on the line in support of either Galileo or his upstart detractor, Horký. Instead, even though many of them had actually seen detailed images of the moon in great magnification, and had seen Jupiter's moons with their own eyes, they yet preferred to wait for others to courageously step forward and verify Galileo's findings. "After all," some of them thought, "who am I to risk taking food out of my family's mouths? And who am I to risk angering the Inquisition with new ideas and discoveries dangerous to the Church?" Truly, above the European land mass clung potent vestiges of the black cloud of the Dark Ages.

So, desperately driven to find support for his anti-Galilean tirades, Horký published a book in Modena full of flimsy, spiteful diatribes against Galileo and his ideas. At the end of it, he concluded, "The only use of Galileo's Medicean Stars is to gratify Galileo's thirst for gold and to make himself the subject of much discussion and praise." Horký stayed in Modena for a short time to contract with purveyors for his book, so that by the time he returned to Magini's house, word of his book had already spread to Bologna. By then, Magini had recognized the cost of his own fence-sitting, and he unceremoniously threw Horký out of his house. Fearing ostracism by Galileo and his camp, Magini promptly wrote to Galileo that he had nothing to do with Horký's book. Still, Galileo's bitterness about the book took years to dissipate.

Regardless of the scornful barbs aimed at Galileo, Magini's support for his new cosmos steadily grew, augmented by the proliferation of his perspiculli. And with them grew the number of his detractors. Like Horký, they became more vociferous, probably in proportion to the perceived threats to their own cushy sinecures.

In his blind arrogance, Horký was not yet sensible to the book's continuing damage to his reputation. Full of hubris and headed for a fall worthy of Achilles, he sent Kepler a copy.

Leaving Italy for what he hoped would be friendlier climes, he was soon traveling through Prague. There, expecting praise, he knocked on Kepler's door. When Kepler saw him, Horký received a burst of indignation.

"Horký, you fool! Do you know what you've done? You have set back science dozens of years by your damnation of this man's discoveries!" Kepler shouted. Panicked, and realizing his folly in assuming Kepler's position, Horký immediately backpedaled, but to no avail.

Kepler was adamant in his defense of Galileo. He later described the event to him, writing, "After venting my wrath against this scum of a fellow whose obscurity has given him audacity, Horký begged so hard to be forgiven that I have taken him again into favor. But only upon this preliminary condition to which he has agreed: I am to show him Jupiter's satellites and he is to see them and own publicly that they are there."

Horký did so, but he was not yet off the hook. Crossing paths with Horký's retraction of his book was a pamphlet printed by Galileo's student John Wedderburn that decimated Horký's original invalidations to Galileo's work. Added to this was Kepler's *Conversation with the Sidereal Messenger*, that fully supported Galileo's theories. However, Galileo knew this would only further elicit resentment in the cabal arrayed against him. Though the attacks on Galileo continued elsewhere in the astronomy community, he found more solidarity in Kepler. That April, Kepler published *Conversation with the Sidereal Messenger*. If only for a moment, Galileo felt relief.

Chapter Seventeen

To the powerful cabal arrayed against Galileo was added the still greater influence of the Jesuits as well as other triggered prelates in the Church. They all saw in the spirit of Galileo's writings the same inquisitive, unrelenting temper they had already found so inconvenient with Luther and his infamous Reformationist adherents. The alarm became greater every day since Galileo had trained many candidates for professorships in the most celebrated universities of Italy. As for the entrenched holdout academicians, a dangerous aura of enlightenment threatened to engulf them. The light of truth made them cringe. Like terrified cockroaches, they scurried away from it in panic, desperately attacking as they retreated into their sacrosanct shelters and academes.

Wounded by continual attacks, but undeterred in his mission, Galileo knew his enemies were stalking him like panthers ready to pounce upon him anew. Known as the Pigeon League because Colombe, the name of their intellectual leader, meant "pigeon," the group was made up of men with axes to grind, who had convinced the insufficiently informed among the clergy that Galileo's ideas were dangerous heresies. So, with the month of April not yet faded, Galileo hedged his bets and cemented his relationship with his patron, meeting Cosimo in Pisa by show-ing him the satellites of Jupiter through an updated telescope. The joy in Cosimo's eyes at glimpsing Jupiter's moons instantly made up for all Galileo had endured that year.

"Am I looking at what I think I'm looking at, Signor Gali-leo?" Cosimo asked.

"Yes, Your Grace. And in doing so, you have already stepped one foot toward the truth of the world. This shows more courage than many who draw their salaries by pretending to know what they do not," Galileo said.

"Ah, you are so well-spoken, Galileo. Should I keep you within the confines of my court, or should I let you loose on your detractors with sword in hand to slay these dragons of ignorance?"

"Give me the sword, Your Grace, and I will do it gladly." They laughed. "But then I would hang for my sins."

Cosimo stepped away from the telescope, still beaming from what he'd seen. "No, my friend, I will never let you hang when you've brought me such joy and excitement that my heart can barely contain."

A servant brought them wine. "Your Grace," Galileo said, "you have already favored me with the honor of sending my book to the kings and princes of Europe under your aegis. I'm wondering, is there a way to bear your influence upon the Church Fathers to—"

Cosimo's face darkened with fear. "You know I can't do that. They hold too much power." Tears of compassion sprang to Cosimo's eyes. "I have no armor for such a battle. As much as my heart is heavy for you, Galileo, that's a favor no man can ask."

～

All that late spring and summer, the thinkers of Europe eagerly watched and read as Galileo, with renewed vigor, continued to build his reputation as the Christopher Columbus of the starry skies. Galileo swept onward, propelled by the momentum of his own fame, sailing his theories successfully through the shark-infested waters of one vitriolic public debate after another. It didn't matter whether the debates centered on the properties of floating bodies, priority of discovery of sunspots, the Ptolemaic versus the Copernican "world systems," or the phases of Venus, which had already shattered the generally accepted Ptolemaic system. However, as fall approached, even darker storm clouds coalesced on the horizon of Galileo's future.

In the midst of those brooding clouds, Galileo's attention turned to his daughters' futures. Of illegitimate birth, lacking sufficient dowries, and somewhat homely as Virginia and Livia were, they had virtually no chance of being considered marriageable. Galileo knew their futures at court were dim. His girls were more likely to wind up as lonely, impoverished spinsters than as the fortunate wives of well-connected courtiers. Galileo struggled with a critical decision—he dearly loved his daughters but could hope for no better futures for them than life in a convent. His mother had seen to that by denying their legitimacy.

Virginia was only ten years old, and Livia nine. Neither of them met the minimum age requirement for a girl to enter a convent, but Galileo was prepared to wait for intervention, divine or otherwise. He called the girls into his study one night and told them they would soon be moving with him to Florence and that he would be leaving their mother, Marina, behind in Pisa to take care of his four-year-old son, Vincenzo. They both cried at the news of imminent separation from their mother as well as abandonment to the world of adults.

But knowing that Galileo had only the best intentions for their futures, they soon resigned themselves to their fate. Virginia, the most proactive of the two, calmly and graciously went about helping her father prepare for the move. Livia lagged behind her sister, as she usually did in such things.

One day, Galileo gently took Virginia aside. "Gina, you know how much I cherish you in my life, don't you?" he asked.

"*Sì, Papà,*" Virginia said.

"Livia is always sickly. She's been so since she came out of her mother's womb. I'm counting on you to take good care of her, because soon your mamma won't be around, and you're not only the older sister, but the more dependable one."

She modestly sidestepped this compliment. "*Papà,* I love Livia, so it's very natural that I will take good care of her."

"Ah, spoken like a grown-up!"

"*Grazie, Papà,*" she said, blushing in modesty.

"Ah, light of my eyes, I love you so!" He hugged her tightly.

"I love you too, *Papà.*" Virginia drew away, shyly smiling back at him as she left the room.

Virginia had a precocious tendency to show consideration, care, and compassion for those she loved. And she loved Galileo more than anyone. Even at the age of ten, she was intelligent enough to appreciate the momentous discoveries he was making and what their ramifications were for the world outside their house. She respected him all the more for that, even though her first stirrings of respect, if not compassion, for another human being were elicited in her feelings for her mother, whom she felt had risen above her flawed background to make a home and family for Galileo.

But as for the respect and admiration Virginia held for him, no one Virginia knew could ever rise to that level in her heart.

Certainly not her mother, whose less than savory past Virginia had accidentally discovered as she helped Galileo prepare for her move to Florence. Virginia sifted through a box of family papers one day and happened upon a copy of the *Catalogue of All the Principal and Most Honored Courtesans of Venice*. Worse yet, she found her own mother's name in the catalogue!

She asked around the neighborhood to find out what a courtesan was, and was shocked to learn it meant a sex worker. Intuiting that this would be a highly sensitive subject to ask either of her parents about, she asked Galileo's mother to shed some light on the subject. Giulia was stunned at seeing the catalogue and at hearing Virginia's query, but recovered herself sufficiently to answer with some diplomacy. She explained that before Marina met Galileo, she worked as a sort of entertainer for men of means, having interesting conversations with them, for pay, to pass their otherwise idle hours.

Giulia couldn't resist the temptation to divulge a further revelation: Sometimes those conversations turned to more intimate experiences. Virginia was highly offended. This explained much that had mystified her about her parents' relationship, and necessarily lowered Marina in her eyes such that any loss she felt when she moved to Florence was greatly softened. After that, all her love was focused on her father. When Marina died within two years of their departure, the loss further removed her from her daughter's heart. As for Galileo, his heart was stung when he heard of Marina's death. Years of constant badmouthing from his mother about her had taken its toll on his affections for Marina.

As Galileo settled in to life in Florence, it is doubtful if, in the early months of 1611, he would have continued to pursue his grander course of advocating for heliocentrism, or that he would have allowed his camp followers to do so, had he been fully cognizant of a dark destiny drawing nearer. Galileo was trifling with a rattlesnake. Cesare Cremonini, another unorthodox academician, had come under the magnifying glass of the Inquisition. Always quick to sniff for hints of heresy, the Inquisitors were also investigating links between Cremonini and Galileo. But, finding nothing of significance on Galileo, they moved on.

Chapter Eighteen

The more Galileo wrote, spoke, lectured, and taught—espousing the controversial Copernican narrative that the Earth and other planets revolved around the sun—the more he angered senior prelates. The credibility of their careers, as well as that of the Roman Catholic Church, hinged on the narrative that God had created man on Earth as the center of the universe, and had placed man on a planet singularly abundant with life around which the entire Cosmos naturally revolved. It did not matter to them that Cardinal Bellarmine had requested the Collegio Romano of the Church to certify Galileo's discoveries, nor that the collegio assented.

One of those angered clerics was Lodovico Colombe, whose last name was incidentally Italian for "pigeon." In his opposition to Galileo's ideas on cosmology and floating bodies, Colombe had amassed a significant following, mindless parrots though they were. Galileo, ever the wag, referred to them as the Pigeon League, owing to their unintelligent mouthing of Colombe's predigested Aristotelian quotations. Aptly named, Galileo's moniker stuck like glue.

The fact that Galileo had no hard proof of his alternative cosmology only strained his mental faculties harder to convince the Pigeon League of it. In return, this only made those opponents harangue him and his intellectual arrogance louder while they organized themselves into cabal after cabal, artfully arrayed against his very existence.

In early 1611, Galileo was in the throes of another controversy that threatened his burgeoning fame. He had just announced a theory that the phases of Venus, revealed by his perspicullum, proved Venus orbited the sun. The fireworks set off by his latest Copernican "scientific heresy" were heard across Europe. But his findings could not be refuted, no matter how many Ptolemaic twistings of flawed logic to save the appearances his opponents pulled out of their hats—or elsewhere.

In late February, Galileo had planned a trip to Rome. Cosimo alerted his Roman ambassador, Piero Guicciardini, to treat Galileo as an official envoy, writing that every one of Galileo's needs should be met while he stayed in Cosimo's palace there.

But poor health delayed Galileo's expedition until the end of March, when Galileo watchers in Rome saw him press his Copernican argument that the planets, including Earth, revolved around the sun. To this end, he recruited bully pulpits wherever he could find them—and he found many, for prelates and noblemen of good sense alike were attracted to his exciting discoveries.

Moreover, Galileo's indefatigable expectation for one and all to convert to his cause was an amusing delight to his friends, as well as a festering annoyance to his vociferous opponents. One particular confrontation was talked about amongst his friends for days afterwards.

Galileo had had a good day, counting several more influential adherents to his noble cause, when he found himself munching on a piece of cheese during an evening salon at the house of a Roman nobleman. Suddenly, springing upon Galileo like a lion upon a gazelle was an Aristotelian shill named Alphonso Moretti. Moretti ambushed him and carped about Galileo's "apostasy" against Aristotle. Moretti waxed eloquent with various hyperboles, which he ascribed to the questionably omniscient Greek.

"The bookworms of the Pigeon League seem to prefer the dusty scrolls of the ancients to the evidences of their own eyes," Galileo responded. "Anyway, why do you embroil yourself for a man who's been dead for twenty-five hundred years? You call yourself his champion and you hate all but Aristotle's friends. You seem ready to live and die for Aristotle, but I'll wager you don't understand so much as the titles of his chapters." Scattered chuckles arose from nearby guests.

"Do you take Plato for an ignoramus and Aristotle for an ass?" Moretti replied.

"I neither call them asses, nor you a mule. I esteem them as heroes of the world, but when I come across their absurd and contradictory assertions echoed down the ages by unthinking parrots, I will not credit them without sufficient reason."

"Do you dare venture to call me an—"

"Forgive me for inferring your asshood, Signor," Galileo said. The guests laughed and he continued, "But I venture to appeal not to the authority of Aristotle but to that of my own senses."

Moretti mumbled something unintelligible, his mouth seeming to come apart at the hinges. He recovered his coherence. "Tell me this, then: How in God's creation has this supposed myth of Aristotle persisted for these hundreds of years?"

"What myth is that, Signor?"

"That if you drop two stones of different weights—"

"Ahh! You speak of the experiment I conducted from the top of a high building with two stones, one light and one heavy?" Galileo asked. "Well, Moretti, if you had deigned to be present for the experiment and observed it with your own eyes—of course, this would have necessitated removing your nose from between the pages of a dusty book—then you would have noticed the two stones landed at the same moment, regardless of their differences in weight."

"*Bravo!*" shouted several guests.

Another guest said to his companion, "Never a dull moment with Galileo."

"He's always good for a laugh," the other replied.

"Yes, at someone else's expense." They both chuckled.

Moretti, stopped in his tracks by the weight of Galileo's arguments and embarrassed by the presence of Galileo's laughing supporters, could only huff, "Well, we have only your word for that."

Those listening continued laughing at Moretti's paltry rejoinder and went on with their conversations, ignoring him altogether.

A few weeks later, Galileo discussed the attacks from academics with his student Benedetto Castelli, a mathematician and abbot of the Benedictine monastery at Monte Cassino, near Rome.

"Signor Galileo," Castelli said, "I know many professors who feel that, under the weight of your proofs, Aristotle has failed them. They now depend on references in the sacred scriptures of our Lord to justify their astronomical theories. What say you to this?"

"First of all, Benedetto," Galileo replied, "we must put things in proper perspective. These professors of the old opinions of whom you speak have, I'm sorry to say, had their reputations upended by my discoveries. Now they must reconcile themselves to their new situation as students instead of professors. The object of the scriptures was never to teach astronomy. Therefore, such references were only calculated to conform to what the common man accepted as true based on what he had observed with the naked eye about the structure of the universe. Instead, the object of the sacred scriptures is to give mankind information necessary for its salvation that surpasses all human knowledge and that comes from the Holy Spirit. The scriptures teach us how to go to Heaven, not how the heavens go.

"However, I don't believe that the same God who endowed us with senses, speech, and intellect also intended us to neglect the use of these while seeking knowledge of the universe. In fact, so little notice is taken of astronomical matters in the scriptures that none of the planets except the sun and moon—and Venus, under the name of Lucifer—are so much as named there. Therefore, the discussion of natural problems should not begin at the authority of the scriptures but at the authority of sensible experiments and necessary demonstrations."

"Thank you, *professore*. That's what I hoped you would say," Castelli replied.

The fact that Galileo was giving more authority to the naked eye than to the scriptures was completely lost to Castelli, who, notwithstanding his position as abbot, was more of a scientist than a prelate. He should have intuited that Galileo was walking unknowingly into a deadly morass.

Several days later, Galileo received a letter from Kepler about

Francesco Sizzi's just-published book, an attempted debunking of Galileo's discovery of the so-called planets he claimed were orbiting Jupiter. Kepler wrote:

Galileo,

I cannot believe the stupidity of some men who call them-selves astronomers, and who in the same breath proceed with the childish theory of sevens. The astronomer Francesco Sizzi believes everything around us is based on the number seven. In his infantile logic, he maintains that because the human head has seven openings—two nostrils, two eyes, two ears, and one mouth—and because there are seven days in the week, seven metals, etc.—therefore there is no room for any extra planets beyond the seven that have already been discovered! He main-tains that extra planets cannot exist! When I finished laughing, Galileo, I was dismayed to realize that some publisher some-where has taken this idiot seriously.

Galileo also burst out laughing as he read. "God in Heaven, when will these halfwits leave me alone?"

Then his laughter turned to tears as he thought about something from the ancient past. It was often said of Roman gladiators who, after numerous falls and blows, appeared to have given up the fight, "*Cor meum ad ludum perdidit hes*" (he's lost his heart for the game). Like a gladiator battling armored fools, Galileo briefly wondered if his was a worthy contest.

"What have you put me on this Earth for," he spoke aloud to God, "if not to show men the truth of what is around them? Why have you given me this purpose, Lord, that has only given me tears and heartache?"

After a while, Galileo wiped the tears from his cheeks. The grief that had been tearing at his heart had passed, but he knew the respite would last only for a while. Like an indefatigable boxer who withstands harder and harder blows, Galileo wished to himself, and prayed to God, that the relentless hate in the words of his enemies would not destroy him.

His sadness slowly faded from his heart. He wrote back to Kepler:

I'm drowning in a sea of idiots. I have nothing but the truth to save me. Even that may not be enough, except that perhaps God will look down and see that I am not writing to impress, nor to gain gold or attention. The attention is pleasurable and the support and encouragement of the duke is beyond recompense. But in the ultimate, I want only truth to prevail. I want men to have the veils of ignorance pulled from their eyes. I want a day to dawn where new ideas, not born of books but of direct observation and experimentation, are not spit upon but are given the respect they deserve.

A while later, Galileo received Kepler's response: "My good friend, Galileo, just as with the men of the sea, your faith in the Almighty will see you through this tumultuous storm, which will inevitably pass. There are calmer seas ahead for you."

Galileo smiled with hope. He contemplated his numerous friends and could not imagine what he would do without their love, encouragement, and support.

Chapter Nineteen

Several years before the Collegio Romano sought to certify Galileo's findings, in 1603, Prince Federico Cesi had founded a new scientific academy in Rome. Cesi was an independently wealthy, free-spending nobleman and a great admirer of Galileo. Prince Cesi, to the great displeasure of his well-moneyed father, preferred seeking an understanding of the natural world to his father's interests: the Cesis had historically made careers by currying favor with powerful churchmen. This had long since become the family tradition as well as the foundation of its wealth.

Luckily for Cesi, his mother was well-fixed with her own fortune as a member of the Orsini clan, and she preferred to see her son follow his heart rather than his father's will. Thus, Cesi's distinguished Lincean Academy—and its grand total of three members—referred to themselves as lynxes, because the lynx was well-known for its acute vision. Although the Lincean roster was short, the lynxes were long on ambition, aiming for complete knowledge of the world, much as da Vinci had dreamed of it a hundred years before.

Thus, in 1611, as soon as Cesi heard about the Collegio Romano vindicating Galileo's findings, and about the grand banquet they had held for him, he decided to induct Galileo as the academy's fourth member. The happy occasion occurred in April at a formal presentation and dinner in Galileo's honor. That night, dressed in his finest attire, Galileo took a coach to Palazzo Corsini, headquarters of the Lincean Academy. He was greeted effusively at the door by Cesi himself, who had quickly become a good friend.

"First, we have the speeches in the great hall," Cesi said, "followed by a banquet and music in the grand salon, both of which have been specially decorated for the occasion."

"You do me a great honor, Federico," Galileo said.

"And don't let me forget to tell you the word I have coined to reflect the singularity of your star-seeking instrument," Cesi said into Galileo's ear.

"Ah," said Galileo, "that shall be my dessert for the evening."

"Not if my chef has anything to say about it!"

They laughed as they entered the grand hall of Palazzo Corsini. In Cesi's eyes, Galileo had certainly become a great man of science, worthy of the hall's festive decorations. His heart leapt when many of the audience members recognized and cheered Galileo.

Cesi escorted his guest of honor to a central chair on the dais in the palazzo's grand hall, where Galileo was met by resounding cheers from the multitude of guests, numbering well over a hundred and including not only the other three Linceans, but also their numerous family members, invited guests, guests of invited guests, and hangers on.

Cesi clinked a crystal water glass to bring silence. "Ladies and gentlemen," he said, "as guests of the Lincean Academy, I want to welcome you all to this auspicious occasion, the induction of Signor Galileo Galilei into our society." As applause followed, Cesi picked up a rolled parchment resembling a diploma and spread it out for the benefit of the audience. "With this certificate, we hereby welcome Signor Galileo Galilei to the Linceans!" He handed the parchment to Galileo, who took it, embraced Cesi, and kissed him on both cheeks.

The applause repeated with more enthusiasm, after which Cesi continued, "Signor Galilei has devoted his life to the cause of science and philosophy, never resting a day without exploring some new corner of knowledge unknown to lesser mortals. His discoveries have not only advanced our knowledge of the heavens, but have shown us what our potential is: to know everything under the sun. Thinking back to Ecclesiastes's famous words, without meaning any offense whatsoever to our Holy Mother Church . . ." Cesi nodded to Claudio Acquaviva, Superior General of the Collegio Romano, who sat on the dais and who, by his very presence that night, signified his agreement with Galileo's theories—not necessarily a very bold move, as the Collegio had already blessed Galileo's discoveries. Cesi continued, "It was Ecclesiastes who said, 'There is nothing new under the sun.' I'm here to inform all of you that there *is* something new under the sun. And his name is Galileo!"

Hearty applause filled the hall, whereupon Cesi asked Galileo to say a few words. Galileo stood, nodded acknowledgment to Cesi, and smiled broadly to the audience. He cleared his throat and took a sip of wine.

"My esteemed colleagues and honored guests," Galileo said, "I heartily thank Signor Cesi for his kind introduction, which I will endeavor to live up to. Before I say a few words, I ask us all to bow our heads in silent reverence for a moment, to honor the memory of the death of very old, outmoded ideas whose time has come to receive proper burial in the annals of modern science.

"Those of you who are acquainted with the struggles I've gone through in recent years: struggles with gentlemen of dubious motives who refused to even look through my spectacle glass. Those of you who *did* dare look at the new stars and moons I have discovered—stars and moons that have sundered forever the old erroneous theories and misunderstandings of the world beyond this Earth—and those of you who have affectionately named me the Starry Messenger after the title of my book. Those of you who know deep in your hearts and minds that the old must inevitably give way to the new. All of you will understand why I am here, why I will never give up my struggle to bring knowledge to man of that which surrounds us all. You will understand why I persist in this seemingly hopeless task when the barbs of ignorant men sting me to the heart and why I try to laugh at their attempts to reject, to disprove, to scoff at the world around them, right in front of their faces." Galileo paused. "They will not look!

"But if those men will only set aside their fears about losing their importance and their well-paying jobs—which exist only to defend a set of two-thousand-year-old theories, admittedly created by a great philosopher named Aristotle, who could only look at the heavens with his naked eyes—they too will see what we have seen in the heavens. They will see that the heavens are far more extensive and far more populated by other strange, new, and unknown worlds than any one of us, even myself, could have ever imagined."

The hall was silent. The audience waited, enraptured, to hear what would come next from Galileo. He went on.

"I stand before you tonight, with my fellow Linceans, to invite you to join me in this quest simply to know what surrounds us." Galileo looked over at Father Acquaviva. "To be sure all the stars, planets, and moons are God's miraculous works.

And so I ask you: Should we not seek to understand God in all his works? Should this effort not reward us with even greater love and understanding for our creator? Is there anyone among you who would disagree with my earnest and innocent goal? I thank you all for listening to the humble entreaties of a man who simply wishes to know, and I raise my glass to honor those who came before us and those who will follow after us—the men who wish to know."

The audience stood, raised their glasses, and cheered. Their applause did not let up until Cesi stood, quieted them, and exhorted them to enjoy the rest of the evening. Galileo was congratulated all round by those on the dais; even Father Claudio, the head of the Collegio Romano, bent to whisper in his ear, "Galileo, you have my full support in your endeavors and I trust this foolish antagonism you have stirred up in some quarters of my college will go the way of the mildewed volumes of which you speak."

Galileo smiled and pressed his hand. "From your lips to the Lord's ears, Father," he said.

Never one to neglect an opportunity to convert kindly faces into acolytes for his cause, Galileo stepped down from the dais to glad-hand the congratulators and the well-wishers who surrounded him. Praise flowed from the mouths of the guests. Having suffered so much from the onslaughts of his detractors, Galileo smiled this way and that, basking in the glory of the moment.

To describe what the lucky guests ate as they reveled in true Italian style would be to rattle off a litany of the finest variety of game to be had on the peninsula. The heads of bear, wild boar, and nine-pointed stag lined the walls of the hall, manifesting the prince's father's fondness for the hunt. Happily, the young prince had inherited the services of experienced deerstalkers, trappers, fishermen, and fowlers from his father, and their professional offerings were abundantly manifested on the tables: the choicest cuts of wild game—boar and stag—from the Silvan and Ciminian Forests; prized veal; suckling pig and aged beef from local farmers; and whole, baked Florentine ring-necked pheasants, which pointed their long, graceful tails proudly upright even above the exquisite flower arrangements adorning the long tables.

The prince's fishermen were not to be outdone—they had brought the cooks a multitude of trout as well as immense Adriatic sturgeon, gently baked in champagne with garlic, thyme, and bay leaves, now being picked apart and devoured with enthusiasm by the guests. All this to celebrate Galileo and his discoveries. Even Galileo, who had by now sat at countless heavily laden tables with noblemen and women, was impressed by such style and abundance.

Cesi, the consummate host, waited patiently while pleasantries were exchanged between Galileo and the guests at his and Galileo's end of their table. Cesi was about to excitedly share something with Galileo when Galileo himself suddenly burst out, "This dinner reminds me of the time Father Tozzetti of Lucca in Tuscany was being honored at his retirement dinner after twenty-five years in the parish."

Galileo spoke so earnestly that only some nearby guests recognized the mock seriousness of his tone, heard at other parties they had attended with him, and knew perfectly well what was coming. They smiled with the gleaming eyes of children about to devour a dessert. Regardless, Galileo had the attention of everyone within hearing distance.

He continued: "A certain leading local politician and

member of the congregation, whose name I've forgotten, was chosen to make the presentation to Tozzetti and give a speech at the dinner. However, the politician was delayed, so Father Tozzetti said his own few words while they waited. 'My first impression of the parish came naturally from the first confession I heard that day,' Tozzetti said. 'From this, I thought I had been assigned to a terrible place. The first person who entered my confessional admitted that when he was young and struggling for money, he had stolen a gold-plated crucifix from the altar of the very church in which we sat that day . . .'"

A shocked and scandalized ejaculation erupted from a Signora Caetano nearby. Galileo spoke on. "'And, when questioned by the police, he was able to lie his way out of it. He went on to confess that he had habitually stolen money from his aging and sickly parents; he had embezzled from his first employer, a wheat merchant, who had seen fit to give him his first chance at a job, then he thanked him by engaging in a tempestuous affair with the merchant's wife! Not only that, but he had almost irretrievably damned himself by seducing his kindly boss's innocent seventeen-year-old daughter. His sins were endless—he had drunk many times to semi-conscious excess and consequently had done shameful things in public he had been told about the next day. He went on and on! He had boasted to himself and to his intimate friends that he had cuckolded many men in the parish, having had numerous illicit affairs with various married women, and this was quite plausible as he was rakishly handsome. He told me that, while drunk, he had been arrested for public nudity.'"

Scandalized, Signora Caetano left the room in a huff. For dramatic purposes, Galileo imitated several gasps from the imagined female guests at the priest's dinner. Then he continued recounting the priest's words: "'I was appalled that one person could do so many awful things. But as the days and months went on, I learned that the people of my parish were not all like that and I had indeed come to a fine parish full of good and loving people.'"

By now, the remainder of the guests had moved from their chairs and crowded around Galileo to hear his story.

"Just as Father Tozzetti finished his talk," Galileo said, "the very anxious but still dignified politician arrived full of apologies for being late. I should add that this man was a well-respected politician in the community whose wife was very ill, such that he found only understanding and forgiveness in the eyes of the guests. So, he immediately began his talk: 'I'll never forget the first day Father Tozzetti came to our humble parish,' said the politician. 'In fact, I had the honor of being the first person to go to him for confession.'"

It seemed as if the salon's walls might not withstand the great vibrations of raucous laughter, table-pounding, whoops, hollers, and cacklings the like of which the servants had never before heard in that great house. The servants, of course, forgot the dictates of decorum and laughed heartily with the rest. One male guest laughed so hard, he was forced to excuse himself in great embarrassment.

Just when a semblance of calm settled in the room and people had caught their breaths after paroxysms of laughter, Galileo, ever the master of timing and with mock sanctimoniousness, piously intoned, "The moral of that story is: never, ever be late."

Soon, appetites comfortably renewed after sitting through the speeches, the guests resumed their bacchanalian pleasures, gorging on whatever was at hand, including steaming *linguini con sarde a mare* from a Sicilian recipe respectfully appropriated from the chef's sardine-loving grandmother.

As Cesi devoured the linguini, he suddenly stopped, forkful of noodles midair, and looked at Galileo, who was focused on doing away with a large portion of sturgeon and a hefty plate of sardine linguini. "Galileo, my good friend, I have a special gift for you tonight," Cesi said.

Galileo's mouth, too stuffed to utter anything halfway intelligible, emitted only a questioning grunt.

"Yes, Your Magnificence," Cesi said, the sweet prosecco going to his head, "I am going to submit for your critical judgment—" Cesi halted to burp, loosened his belt, then resumed. "For your critical judgment, I shall submit to you the perfect word for your spectacle glass! This word, which I've coined just yesterday—" He burped again. "—For your spectacle glass, yes! I've coined this word in order to properly distinguish your instrument from that simple child's toy of the Dutchman Lippershey. Thus, your glass is henceforth to be referred to as—" He burped a final time. "As . . . the telescope!"

Of course, Galileo did not know that an obscure student of astronomy, Giovanni Demisiano, aware of the spectacle glass, had found the existing terminology wanting and coined the word *telescopio* only months before. He had written to Cesi about it, and Cesi, still in his twenties and wanting to share in Galileo's limelight, had announced it as his own.

Galileo, interest piqued, swallowed a mouthful of linguini a bit too quickly. He pulled a slight, yet annoying, sardine spine from his tongue, set it discreetly on the tablecloth under his plate, and asked, quite pleased, "What is this term?"

Cesi grinned. "It's a new word, I tell you. In our Italian

language. Your wonderful spectacle glass is henceforth—of course, you must like it!—to be called not a spectacle glass, but a *telescope.*"

A hush came over the nearby guests as they waited for Galileo's response.

Sobered but for a moment, Galileo pondered the new word. "Marchese Federico, in one stroke, you have outdone yourself as well as outshone the sages of the ink and quill."

Cesi nodded. "Thank you, kind sir."

Galileo continued, "I suspect you have combined the Greek words 'tele,' meaning 'far off,' with 'scopein,' 'to look at.' And thus, we have the new word *telescope*—'to see far off.' Am I right?"

Federico nodded again. "*Certo.*"

"*Bravo* and brilliant, Marchese!" said Galileo. "Your generosity is surpassed only by your intelligence. I am grateful. My spec—my *telescope* has tonight been officially christened!"

With that, "telescope" was repeated from one guest to the next down the length of the host's table. Crossing over to the parallel tables, "telescope" sailed newly hatched around the room. Venetian Murano goblets were raised in numerous inebriated toasts to Galileo's telescope. Needless to say, *l'evento Galileo,* along with its amusing anecdote, were the talk of Rome's high society in the following days.

Chapter Twenty

But by the time Galileo returned to Florence, all was not so rosy. Toward the end of the year, Galileo received a letter from a painter friend in Rome:

Signor Galileo,

I have been told by a friend, a priest who is very fond of you, that a gang of men, envious of your virtue and merits, met at the residence of the Archbishop of Florence, seeking some means by which to damage you, either with regard to the motion of the Earth or otherwise. One asked the preacher Tommaso Caccini to state from the pulpit that you were asserting outlandish things. The priest, seeing the animosity against you, replied as a good Christian and a member of the respected and powerful Dominican Order ought. I write so that your eyes may be open to the envy and malice of these evildoers.

Over the next several years, as Galileo's fame grew, so did the simmering cauldron of hate, envy, and anti-Galilean propaganda fueled in part by one contingent of Dominican friars. The friars were popularly known as Hounds of the Lord, as much for the pun on their name (*Domini Canes*) as for their unrelenting zeal in fighting heresy. This antipathy toward Galileo and his ideas was nowhere as intense as in Florence, which was home to a number of narrow-minded zealots. One morning, while Galileo washed his face, he looked at himself in the mirror and shuddered at how different he appeared, even from one or two years earlier. His face had become heavily, unnaturally lined—even disfigured. He looked like a tortured individual. The stress of the verbal and written attacks he had so far endured was taking its toll on his features.

Not only that, but he had lately developed sleep problems. The relentless onslaught of diatribes had set painfully in his mind like implacable, viciously barbed fish hooks and would not leave him alone. He was never well-rested. Between his long working hours and the constant attacks, he tossed and turned at night, trying to sleep in the midst of a throbbing headache, with voices coming to him, intoning choice phrases from the onslaughts of the week. Not even strong drink could shut up the voices.

"Galileo's theories are the pathetic and fanciful imaginings of a twisted mind."

"Galileo has managed, in one broad stroke, to pervert the well-intentioned qualities of science, scripture, and philosophy."

One invective that particularly stung him and plagued him day and night came from a vicious prelate: "I pray there be a special place in hell for those such as Galileo who would sweep away, in their vanity and their grasping for gold, the trusted truths of our Sainted Church Fathers."

These curses swam in his fevered mind. Coupled with his physical ailments and their attendant pains, the onslaught made him feel he could go on no longer. But somehow, he rose each morning to tackle a new day. The one joy in his life was his daughter Virginia. He had for years nicknamed her Gina out of tenderness for his favorite daughter, who returned his love with unconditional admiration.

In 1613, Galileo was greatly relieved when he received special dispensation for his daughters to enter the convent of San Matteo in nearby Arcetri. His girls got used to the privations of this convent of Poor Clares, an order notorious for the poverty of its nuns. Galileo visited his daughters daily, bringing them sufficient sustenance and a little money to supplement their meager existence. Every time he came to the convent, he depended on Gina to cheer him up. He was comforted too by the letters Gina wrote to him between his visits. She was his daughter, but as a mother would, she took pains to ensure his happiness however she could. From Gina, Galileo received the sort of care and concern the outside world rarely gave him. In short, they were devoted to each other. In contrast, his own mother had, in his childhood, dragged him before the Inquisition for calling her names. In later life, had spied on him to learn if he was going to mass and had actually physically attacked his mistress, Marina. This caused an irreparable rift between them which was solidified when Giulia refused to let her son marry Marina.

Heartened by the hope of new astronomical discoveries to be made and of future patrons who could muzzle his detractors with their power and influence, Galileo pressed on, straight into the teeth of the omnipotent forces arrayed against him. He was David, charging not one, but a phalanx of Goliaths. Yet he knew God listened to his prayers and was on his side—how could he lose? If nothing else, his faith drove him forward, day after painful day. He felt as if his tears were eroding canyons in his face.

He knew with chilling certainty that his pursuit might mean his eventual death at the hands of the Inquisitors, who had already burnt the outspoken "unrepentant heretic" Giordano Bruno in Rome and who had knocked ominously on Cesare Cremonini's door.

The Inquisition was Galileo's sword of Damocles, but he didn't care. This was his life. This was Galileo.

Chapter Twenty-One

Among the mental pygmies of the Pigeon League, a Dominican named Niccolò Lorini had the dubious honor of being the first friar to attack Galileo from the pulpit, spewing forth his harangue at Galileo's expense. But in the week following, Lorini incurred such an uproar from Galileo's friends, some in the form of complaints to the Dominican hierarchy, that Lorini was forced to write a public letter of apology, which by its very nature vindicated Galileo's ideas.

However, such an apology as that served only to hasten the resolve of a fellow Dominican Hound, Cosimo Caccini, who soon evolved into Galileo's nemesis. Raised in the crucible of sixteenth-century Dominican monastic life, Caccini was a self-styled combination of St. Thomas Aquinas and Girolamo Savonarola—after all, Savonarola had risen to fame with his bombastic, hateful sermons in the same San Marco monastery that had spawned Caccini.

Later on, however, Caccini's zeal matured. Not wishing to meet the same horrible fate as his predecessor—whose Draconian strictures had led him to the fiery stake—Caccini glibly changed his given name from Cosimo to Tomasso after his patron saint. Inside, he shifted his true allegiance to Savonarola.

And as this man with a plan had hoped, Caccini's reputation over the years had grown from that of a simple Dominican novitiate to a determined Hound of the Lord, known as he was for being a staunch *evisceratrice dal pulpito* ("eviscerator from the pulpit"). To be fair, there was a certain drama to his showmanship, to his unrelenting condemnation of anything even vaguely resembling heretical thought. As such, his sermonizing, always calculated to "fire up the pews," was frequently requested in the Tuscan province, and later in Rome, as his reputation warranted.

Thus was Caccini offered the chance of his otherwise unremarkable career: a sermon from none other than Filippo Brunelleschi's lofty, vaunted pulpit at Santa Maria Novella in Florence. For this, the eviscerator would set his sights on the heresy of Galileo Galilei. And if Caccini made good here, he intuited that Rome would be his next assignment. The prospect thrilled him to the marrow. From this rampart in Santa Maria, Caccini would hand down his electrifying commandments in the resounding tones of a latter-day Moses. By this point, he had indeed set himself as the rightful descendant of so many Church Fathers or progenitors that he could barely keep track of them all. Yes, he thought, the occasion called for none other than the imagined blazing oratory of Moses.

And so Father Tomasso Caccini became Florence's chief anti-Galilean propagandist. True to that description, early on the morning of the fourth Sunday of Advent, December 20, 1614, he strolled purposefully toward the entrance of the Church of Santa Maria Novella.

His resolute steps took him past the ancient obelisks that had marked the chariot races of the Roman circus, just as they had been marking the more modern chariot races instituted by a former duke of Florence. The grand obelisks reminded

Caccini that he was living in dangerous times, which naturally required great deeds of high courage.

Emboldened by the idea, Caccini entered the church and glanced up at the distinctive white marble façade executed by Alberti during the High Renaissance. Caccini mulled over his morning sermon as he passed impressive works by Botticelli, Ghiberti, Brunelleschi, Lippi, Ghirlandaio, and Masaccio. But he paid them not the slightest attention. On his mind was the future of his chosen nemesis, Galileo.

Today, I will show Signor Galilei once and for all that his fate is in my hands, he thought, as he barely acknowledged the greetings of parishioners who had packed the pews in expectation of his talk.

It had come down to this: Caccini was ruthlessly determined to make a name for himself over the lifeless remains of Galileo's reputation. Such career-advancing machinations as these excited Caccini's mind to creative heights and easily took precedence over such relative insignificances as the lack of a sufficient dowry for an upcoming marriage, or the possible, even likely, cuckolding of an irate parishioner. Caccini sensed his own instrumentality in Galileo's fate and theorized that he could easily curry favor with Rome by nailing Galileo to the proverbial cross of heresy on this most auspicious morning. As he considered his forthcoming success in Rome, Caccini sneered to himself, "My star will finally rise, just as Galileo's star sinks into the Tiber."

With a smug expression, he sat down on a bench in the sacristy, underneath a della Robbia masterpiece, and memorized his sermon. The chattering of the faithful in the pews outside did not disturb him. He would soon stir them to righteous indignation and word would spread all the way to Rome of the outrage of the faithful.

Minutes later, likening himself to the avenging archangel St. Michael, Caccini took an aggressive stance at Brunelleschi's imposing marble pulpit. He began his sermon, crowing like a cock over what he dared fantasize would be the shattered body of Galileo, broken on the Inquisitor's wheel. Such happy thoughts as these filled his mind as his pious words cracked like lightning bolts from the pitiless sky above Mount Ararat.

"My faithful, my dear brethren and sisters, whom I have given my life to serve and to save as best I can from the sins of the world, from eternal damnation, and to deliver your souls into the hands of our Lord leading to the everlasting glory of Heaven. I come to you today to speak of a grave matter at hand in the streets and halls of our city and in the fields of the farms wherever thinking men trod the ground of Tuscany.

"Here, there is daily evidence of a façade of faith! A façade of obeisance to the will of God! A façade of following and trusting the word of God as written down by the prophets, our first fathers of the Holy Church! You might very well ask yourselves, 'Who builds these façades to worship the Lord? Who dares profane His holy love with this sacrilege?' Do you want to know, my brethren?"

Several hearty yeses rang out in the nave.

Caccini responded, "I will tell you of one who would have you believe the Earth revolves around the sun!"

There were several guffaws in the pews. "It's not true!" someone shouted.

Caccini, warming to his Greek chorus, replied, "Yes, he would have you believe that, as he offers his calculations in one hand like the apple in the Garden of Eden! 'Eat of this apple, partake and believe in this knowledge I share with you, and surely you will enter paradise.' He profanes further yet! He says to you, 'Who needs the word of God when truth is right before you? Just look through this tube and you will see the ultimate truth.' What this man Galileo calls his discoveries are nothing but his crimes against the Almighty, which truly merit the vengeance of Heaven!

"When Joshua prayed to God to stop the sun from moving in the day, to keep the day so that the Israelites might see their enemies to slay them, who was it who had faith in the Israelites? Who was it who stopped the sun from moving in the sky? Who was it who showed man that the sun revolves around us every day? It was God, my faithful friends! It was not Galileo, who has the blasphemous effrontery to tell us what the sun does when God has *already* told us! It was God!

"And I invite Signor Galileo to stand before this congregation and challenge the word of God, instead of hiding behind his stacks of books and papers of asinine astronomical calculations that don't amount to the significance of an anthill when faced with God's light, God's truth, and God's revelations to the prophets. *These* are truths everlasting!"

It was here that Caccini's high-pitched voice, raised almost to a scream, disturbed the concentration of a fellow Dominican, Alberto Giordano, who was reciting a novena to himself in a basement office. Irked by this disturbance, and knowing this was Caccini's first sermon at the church, Giordano quietly climbed the stairs all the way to the choir so as not to disturb the orator. He sat unobtrusively in a back corner of the choir and listened, more out of curiosity about the excitement than anything else. He had been charged with reporting to an officer of the order as to Caccini's performance that day, but had not taken the command seriously.

As Giordano listened, he grew somewhat concerned for

the reputation of Santa Maria Novella. Savonarola's fate, after all, was anything but forgotten among either the faithful or the clergy of Florence. And given Giordano's advanced years, the memories of Savonarola's sermons still lingered in his mind.

Looking out upon the congregation, he suddenly noticed the visage of Monsignor Luciano Montefiore of the Holy Office. *Ah,* he thought, *the Holy Office must already have its eye on this fatuous fool. If there is anything to be concerned about, Montefiore, the loyal Hound, will see that the matter is resolved.*

There was no love lost between himself and either Caccini or Montefiore. Many times he had wished them a quick journey to hell in a handbasket, then chided himself remorsefully. Giordano looked upon Caccini as a transparent opportunist, and upon Montefiore as a useless attachment to an even more useless but dangerous bureaucracy, which caused more pain than revelation to prelates and parishioners alike.

With this conclusion about Caccini, Giordano rose and returned to the basement to continue his novena. Caccini had not noticed him and went on with his diatribe:

"And where will Galileo's spectacle glasses and papers be when he, at the end of his puny life, stands before the judgment of the Lord, the Holy Ghost, the host of Heaven? Where will they be, the leavings of his paltry, self-serving life? They will be rotting in the dirt of his grave, along with Galileo. Being eaten by worms! And then, after all his vain utterings, will Galileo be at the mercy of the Lord on the day of judgment. For it is God who moves the Earth! It is God who commanded the sun to stop at midday, so that the Israelites might smite their enemies. And it is God to whom we will answer on the day of judgment. It will never be Galileo!"

Another unfortunate listener that morning was Alessandro

Marino. A loyal Galileo follower, he had heard of Caccini and, motivated by protective intent, had decided to monitor whatever came out of Caccini's mouth concerning his scientific mentor. But this tirade was too much for his sensitive heart to take. Caccini's hateful words cut like a scythe through his mind and his heart. Someone he revered was being torn to ribbons in front of his very eyes. Marino fantasized about what he would say to the man at the pulpit. "You, who do not measure up to Galileo's ankles, have yet the gall to tear him down to your pitiful level. You, who have the greatness of a toad, will never know how true a heart has Galileo to the pursuit of truth. Damn you!"

But he knew he would not stand up and call out in rage, so he did the one thing of which he was able: he got up and walked out. *I hope one and all see me leave this nave, made a temporary hellhole by this gutter scum*, he thought.

Monsignor Montefiore was also squirming in his seat. Momentarily distracted by Giordano's exit, he focused again on what spewed from Caccini's untiring mouth and vocal cords. Montefiore had been given the task of monitoring any covertly voiced, heretical, Reformation-type attitudes coming from the lesser prelates of the Dominican Order. Pope Paul V appreciated the Dominican's Counter Reformation zeal, but as popes would, Montefiore thought, this particular pope carefully withheld his full trust from *everyone*, from the Dominicans to members of the Holy Office.

But now, Montefiore's patience was finally being tried, and irritated, he began to think of Caccini as a poor parody of himself. Montefiore took a deep breath and calmed down. He knew his superiors at the Holy Office, if they could have been privy to his thoughts, might have chastised him for overreacting. But he still wished he could escape the nave. He had heard many better sermons and he was sure this one would incite the opposition, the Galileans. Montefiore concluded that, vitriolic as he was, Caccini was nothing more than a harmless zealot. He stood abruptly and left the church in a hurry.

Caccini glanced back, wondering who was walking out on him, as Montefiore made in haste for the front doors. Too proud to admit of anything lacking on his own part, he mused briefly that the man might have had some pressing commitment elsewhere.

But then there was the young man who had left earlier looking greatly dismayed. Regardless, Caccini comforted himself that his powerful oratory had held the attention, and even the awe, of the vast majority of worshippers that day, and that his sermon would be talked about in the weeks to come as a fine example of Florentine religiosity. Caccini's skills had been honed to a sharp point in the San Marco monastery and, if nothing else, he knew his audience.

Another listener, the corpulent Maffeo Cartoni, had also toyed with leaving. But his wife and three daughters surrounded him in the pew—he would have to drag them out too, causing a scene and disturbing Father Caccini's sermon. And yet, Maffeo felt uneasy about the sermon. His intuition told him there was something not quite right about the man reflected in his sermon, which went on and on with torturous circumlocutions. But as he would always do, this man of substance, a purveyor of wheat and other grains, drowned his intuition in the thought that a greater mind than his had installed Caccini there that day to impart his revelations to the parish. Others would take care of the matter, if indeed there was one.

Caccini's sermon droned on, referencing the Book of Joshua

to drive home his point about the importance of faith over scientific reason. When he felt he had finally gotten this across, Caccini added, "Thus the fools who look for meaning, for truth, for enlightenment, lo, even for salvation—" he laughed, "in God's physical works? In the stars and the planets? These fools who deny the very words of our Lord written down through the hands of the prophets, and instead seek salvation of their souls by looking through tubes filled with glass, who would ascend to Heaven by working their fingers stiff in their astronomical calculations, they place their trust vainly in the idea that God's Earth revolves around the sun! Pure heresy! Yes, I'm speaking of that heretic Galileo and his minions—they are all faithless idiots seeking God in the night sky like a blind beggar looking for gold in a pig sty."

Meanwhile, a relieved Montefiore walked across the piazza fronting the church. His attention shifted from Caccini to Galileo. Of course, he had heard not only of his unconventional theories, but also of the squabblings Galileo had stirred up among numerous conservative prelates and confirmed philosophers of the ancient and unassailable bulwarks of thought. Perhaps there was something to these heretical accusations of Caccini's after all. Without so much as the faintest concern for the ultimate fate of the hapless person who comes to be of interest to the Holy Office, Montefiore resolved to suggest that his superiors look into "this Galileo matter."

This, after all, was his mission in Florence—to ferret out those heretical false believers who hid behind pious facades and scattered their dangerous ideas among the impressionable minds of the populace. Montefiore speculated that word of this sermon would inevitably spread to Rome, and that those faithful to Galileo would react defensively by bringing the matter before the Vatican. Therefore, the politically safest thing to do about it, for Montefiore himself, was what he was already planning to do.

I'll just set the investigators of the Holy Office on Galileo's trail and see what they turn up, Montefiore thought.

An innocent enough initiative and exactly the sort expected of him. Who could blame him for acting thus? Like Pontius Pilate, he mentally washed his hands of the matter.

Part Two

WORLDS COLLIDE

Chapter Twenty-Two

It was a comely morning as Luciano Montefiore made his way across the Piazza di San Pietro toward the Congregation for the Doctrine of the Faith—otherwise known as the Holy Office, or the Supreme Sacred Congregation of the Roman and Universal Inquisition—which was housed along the Piazza del Sant'Uffizio in the Palace of the Holy Office.

The day was not too hot nor too cold, only tentatively cloudy with a promise of unbroken sunshine to come in the afternoon. This expectation pleased those in the streets who made their living on the sidewalks, such as beggars, pickpockets, garbage haulers, street notaries, and various purveyors of fish, fruit, and fowl.

A fine Roman misfit stew, thought Montefiore as he reached the Holy Office, having threaded his way among the patchwork of pedestrians.

The first-floor windows of the palazzo's façade were barred, as if to repel vengeance-minded apostates and heretics. And the twenty-foot solid oaken doors could certainly withstand an angry mob of the same, should the need arise. While the shutters had been opened on the second floor, the morning light favored by the rank and file of the palace, for some oddly non-vampiric reason, sunlight was anathema to the Inquisitors within, such that most of the hallways existed in perpetual darkness. Apparently not too proud of themselves and their activities, which literally brought the fires of hell to the feet of too many of the local citizenry, these same bishops and lesser prelates preferred to save souls in the darkened rooms and basement dungeons of the palace. Unless, of course, they were to save those who had strayed from the faith in local piazzas by offering them the holy light of a bonfire reserved for them.

As Montefiore entered through the imposing arched doors, he looked up at the original architect's pet decoration: a carved marble balcony jutting boldly from the second floor, complete with ornate railing and filigreed capital. Montefiore imagined the pope himself stepping out at the railing to bless the crowds on the Piazza del Sant'Uffizio. The balcony, however, was deserted as Montefiore strode inside to do his doctrinal duty. He went up two flights of stairs and down a long, dark hallway to meet his mentor and superior, Bishop Agostino Filippi, a first-level investigator whose portfolio included looking into the habits and beliefs of scientists, philosophers, men of letters and the arts—arguably, the most dangerous of potential heretics due to their influence over the multitude.

This watchfulness kept Filippi busy, but he always had time to advise his protégé. Montefiore sat and stared at his mentor. Filippi was an abrupt, thin man who, prior to that tumultuous year, had been quite fat. It was either his luck or his curse, depending on his mood, that he had been finishing his sabbatical at the Order of St. John in the southern region of the island of Malta when the Ottoman Turks invaded the island. While taken prisoner and cruelly starved for weeks during the ill-fated assault, it had been Filippi's misfortune to contract an obscure intestinal ailment, possibly dysentery, which had ruthlessly stripped him of his excess weight. It had left him a wraith-like shadow of his former self, and profoundly altered his personality.

Ransomed from his imprisonment by the Dominican Order, which had more funds at its disposal than the Order of St. John, Filippi returned to Florence a changed man. Even his voice had changed. He was no longer the quiet, self-effacing gentleman he had been before his sabbatical. He had become a wiry, abrasive thorn in many sides at the Holy Office. Those above him took into account his recent trauma and simply gave him a wide berth when they passed him in the hallways. Today, Montefiore awaited his mentor's response to his proposal regarding Father Caccini's sermon that morning.

Filippi put Montefiore's papers in order and chuckled at something he read.

"What is this here? You speak of the Church and the State as separate entities?" he asked. "This would be highly amusing if it were not so dangerous. What you think of as the State is us, the Church, as the Holy Father and his Cardinals choose to apply the scriptures to civic affairs. The State is a mere fantasy. The seminary should have taught you your history, Luciano. With the solidification of the authority of the Holy See over the affairs of men, the Church *became* the State. And anything that threatens the power of the State is an enemy to the Church. That's the whole point of the Holy Office—to ensure our power over the affairs of men as guided by the State. After all, it is not us who light the bonfires under the heretics. It's the secular authority."

Montefiore looked dismayed. "I don't understand, Your Excellency," he said.

"We lie beneath the surface of the State, the mechanical

constructions of which have been laid down for us by the politicians whom we own and control utterly, if not in a de jure sense, then in a de facto one," Filippi explained. "Excommunication and eternal damnation are heavy hammers we seldom wield to maintain a state of governmental affairs to the liking of the Vatican.

"Our real job in this building, and therefore *your* job, is to preserve what we have long since formed. We brook no challengers to the power we have accrued. Not challenges from fiery, self-promoting clerics such as Savonarola or Caccini. Nor challenges from scientists, philosophers, or astronomers, such as Galileo, whom I have heard arrogantly ascribes to himself all three such categories. Heresy is nothing more than a challenge to our power. Once you understand this, Luciano, it will make your job much easier."

Filippi took a drink of wine from a tall glass, then continued. "Now, as you go through your daily functions, think of it this way. Even when you come across vitriol from a fiery priest, ask yourself, 'Does his invective challenge our power?' Usually not."

"Our power?" Montefiore asked.

Filippi began to wonder if Luciano had had an attack of stupidity. "Yes, Luciano. You can bask in the certain knowledge that you are part of this. We are the *real* state. Government officials bow to us. We do not bow to them, with the exception of the duke of Tuscany, and even that is a charade. The shopkeepers, the fishmongers, the boatmen on the Arno, the vegetable hawkers in the Piazza di San Pietro, the lawyers in the Via Toselli, even the gonfaloniere in the Hall of the Five Hundred—they all kiss *my* hand. Remember, Luciano, anything that threatens the State is anathema to us and must be reported as heresy."

Filippi looked at his young protégé. "I know, I know, it's a funny little game we play. They challenge our power and we threaten to excommunicate them. That's usually enough to shut them up. Or if they don't shut up, it becomes very simple. We have the State send them to hell in a fireball."

Montefiore looked submissive, even cowed. "I think I understand now, Your Excellency."

Filippi barely nodded in acknowledgment, then continued his rant. "To ensure the State was free of heresy and of lazy misunderstandings about Jesus's teachings, the Holy Church was forced to *become* the State hundreds of years ago. Kings, queens, dukes, duchesses, marquises, marquessas—they're all a pretense. And we take no chances with them; we keep files on anyone of importance in any of the governments and noble classes of Europe. Knowing their misdeeds as we do, it becomes easy to convince them to act with our agenda in mind." Filippi chuckled smugly. "They think they control things. They don't."

Leaning back in his chair, Filippi sighed. "Nevertheless, Luciano, you have put a great deal of thought into this letter to me, although I'm not sure who is to be investigated here—Caccini, for his well-intentioned but clearly opportunistic sermon (we know he's angling for a posting in Rome), or Galileo, for his less than conventional view of the Cosmos."

"Your Excellency, I beg to—" Montefiore started.

"Never beg, Luciano. It degrades the beggar and peeves he who has been begged."

Montefiore looked embarrassed.

"Luciano, it's all about authority," Filippi said. "About power. Savonarola, as you know, attempted to take on the authority of the Holy See and was set aflame for it. He is still burning in hell for it as we speak. Caccini presumes in a not too dissimilar fashion. Is he dangerous to us? Who knows? Time will tell. Meanwhile, we will watch him, but that isn't your department. You are the tip of our spear. As for Galileo, a much simpler figure in the scheme of things, we will most certainly watch him and we will act if he makes the mistake of wading into dangerous waters. If he does, we'll roast him in his own heretical juices."

Filippi gave out a hearty, full-throated laugh, then studied other papers on his desk. Looking up at Montefiore as if he had instantly forgotten his presence in the room, he added, "Luciano, for a number of reasons, you have done a good thing today and this will not go unnoticed on the first and second floors."

But as he exited and crossed the shadowed halls of the Inquisition, Montefiore was not at all sure he had done a good thing. Indeed, he had the sudden creeping sensation that he was walking the hallways of hell. What was the value of human thought, after all? Were men simply pawns to be moved about on a chess board at the pleasure of their masters?

Montefiore felt stifled. He had to get out of that building. When he had made it through the front doors, he felt safe again. Safe from the Hounds who had befriended him and who would never expect him to turn on them. He walked out into the sunshine and the free air. Thus, on a sunny day in Florence, doubt entered Montefiore's mind like an insidious tidal stream subtly eroding the foundation of his faith.

Chapter Twenty-Three

In the meantime, word had spread rapidly about Caccini's diatribe of Galileo, causing furor in some quarters and satisfaction in others. Caccini's brother, Matteo, a cardinal's cup bearer in the Vatican and a self-styled power broker, was appalled at his brother's behavior and chastised him severely in a letter:

It may come to pass that you'll regret ever having learned to read. You fake religion and zeal to cover your animosity, Tommaso. Or was the attack your idea? How thoughtless you have been to let yourself be taken in by those pigeons! You could have done nothing more annoying to the high authorities here. Up to the very highest. It's no use draping yourself with the mantle of religion because everyone knows how you friars use such cover to indulge your ugly passions. Take it from me, brother—reputation rules the world.

And to perform such idiocy at the behest of that nasty Pigeon League just as we were trying to open up a career for you through high protections—rest assured, that has spelled doom for any Roman aspirations you may have harbored! Think where you'd like to go, Tommaso, because you are disliked there and here even more. If you don't find a way to move out, I shall find one for you. You have behaved like a dreadful fool. Tommaso, you have revealed such dreadful plans that I can scarcely control myself. In any event, I wash my hands of you forever.

Possibly, Matteo's ire was brought on by Caccini's damage to the family name. Doubly so due to Matteo's attempts, prior to this fiasco, to gain favor for his brother in Rome.

This should have spelled the end of *l'affair Caccini*, but it was only the beginning. Several days later, Galileo received a note from someone in the Dominican Order who was a friend and ally of Galileo as well as Caccini's superior, and a priest-general in the order. Galileo read:

Signor Galileo,

I beg your forgiveness for the transgression of Friar Caccini at the Church of Santa Maria Novella last month. I feel infinite disgust, especially because the author is a friar of my order. Philosophical and scientific disagreements have no place within the bounds of our Holy Mother Church. We realize you have, in your teachings, meant no harm to us, and we in turn mean no harm to you.

To my great regret, I am responsible for all the bestialities which thirty thousand brothers have done and can do. I knew Caccini, in his mad opportunism, could be manipulated by those Florentine pigeons, but I never would have imagined such craziness as this. In the future, I will not open the door to such impertinence. Though it is spoken from our pulpit, it merely represents the fury of others, not of the Church. We hope you will overlook

Monsignor Caccini's overbearing zeal and lack of discretion in this matter.

Such a letter sufficiently gave Galileo reason to write off the whole brouhaha as a piece of unpleasant history. But it was not to be. Caccini's zeal to destroy Galileo only increased from this reprimand from his superior. Encouraged by the Pigeon League in Florence, working in concert, Caccini and another co-conspirator, Niccolò Lorini, brought formal complaints of heresy against Galileo to the Florentine Inquisition. Not an entity to have knee-jerk reactions, given an atmosphere unfriendly to false heresy accusations, the Inquisitors were nevertheless ultimately forced to take up an investigation of Galileo, a fact that became known to Pope Paul V, who was ever conscious of his image with the cardinals who had elected him.

Caccini had not stopped at malicious, pulpit-born invective, however. No, this self-righteous hypocrite of the cloth had stooped to eavesdropping on suspected heretics. One day, he secretly overheard one of Galileo's students discussing with a Dominican priest the hypothesis that God was an accident. Caccini made the leap of logic to infer that Galileo had taught the student this brand of heresy. Then, when the student mentioned Copernican theory, Caccini interrupted, blurting out that it was heresy to declare the sun stationary, as it was contrary to Holy Scripture.

Unknowingly, Caccini had initiated a chain reaction. Once a formal process had started within the Holy Office, it then had to be followed through with slavish righteousness. In short order, Caccini was deposed by Michelangelo Seghizzi, the Commissary General of the Holy Roman and Universal Inquisition.

Caccini began his diatribe: "With modesty befitting the

office I hold, I preached that holding Copernican theories contradicted the Catholic faith, because such reasoning went against our theologians as well as the Holy Fathers. I then counseled the faithful that no one was allowed to interpret divine scripture contrary to the sense on which all the Holy Fathers agree."

Seghizzi instinctively recognized in Caccini a kindred spirit. They were both out to destroy, their only difference being that Seghizzi, who had originally intended to go into law before choosing the priesthood, was a fastidious detail man. Both he and Caccini loved the thought of burning heretics, but only Seghizzi would think to bring the kindling wood.

"And what are Galileo's ideas regarding the Catholic faith?" Seghizzi asked.

"Many regard Galileo with suspicion in matters of faith because they say he is close to Father Paolo Foscarini, of the Servite Order, famous in Venice for his impieties. And they say letters are exchanged between them even now. There is more, Honorable Commissary General."

Taking notes, a scrivener from the Holy Office struggled to keep up.

"I have seen and read a letter Galileo Galilei wrote to his friend and follower Benedetto Castelli that contains questionable doctrines in the domain of theology. Indeed, some of Galileo's followers believe God was an accident and that the saints never worked miracles," Caccini continued.

"From what sources have you learned this?" Seghizzi asked.

"Sources, Commissary General? For sources, we have much of the Florentine population where Galileo's Copernican ideas are infamous—"

"Names. I require names."

"Well," Caccini hesitated. "There is the misled student I mentioned earlier, who learned his heresies from Galileo."

The complaint was efficiently and diligently taken up, but ultimately was discounted based on the conclusions of the Holy Office consultant who had the foresight to seek an accurate copy of the Benedetto Castelli letter, which contained no heresies compared to the copy presented by Cacccini.

Caccini, sharply chastised for his invectives by his brother, was left with the grim realization that his short-lived foray into notoriety had flopped. This gave rise to Galileo's efforts to neutralize Caccini's damage in a letter to his friend and admirer Monsignor Piero Dini, an influential Vatican official. Galileo also wrote to Grand Duchess Christina, the wife of Cosimo II, who had inquired about this issue at a salon she had recently held. His letter was a treatise defending Copernicanism and was purported to show how Copernicanism was not in conflict with either the scripture or the teachings of the Church Fathers. In and of itself, the letter was a promulgation for the coexistence of science and religion. Tragically, it was not viewed as such by his detractors.

Added to these heliocentrist barbs launched into the hide of the Church was a pamphlet written by Father Paolo Foscarini, who straddled the worlds of religion as a Catholic theologian and a Carmelite prelate, and the world of science as the author of a seven-volume encyclopedia of the liberal arts, physics, and metaphysics. Father Foscarini's pamphlet was addressed to the General of the Carmelite order and was entitled "Letter of opinion over the Pythagorean and Copernican opinion concerning the mobility of the earth and the stability of the sun." Inevitably, the pamphlet wound up on the desk of Cardinal Bellarmine, who at once recognized it as much more contentious than Galileo's letter to Grand Duchess Christina which had argued for both Copernicanism and the peaceful coexistence of science and religion.

As these missives from Galileo circulated in Florence and in Rome, various prelates were drawn reluctantly to one side or the other of the controversy, depending on their education, their native intelligence, their intellectual courage, and their overall integrity. Chief among them was Cardinal Bellarmine. Bellarmine chose his targets carefully, always one to use labor-saving devices where possible. In reaction to the latest scandal, he took care of Galileo and Father Foscarini by writing the same letter to each. Still wishing to tiptoe gingerly around the subject of Copernicanism, Bellarmine diplomatically prefaced his response stating that, should demonstrations ever be made that the Earth moves and the sun stands still, the Holy Mother Church would have to use great caution in its interpretation of scripture that seemed to oppose such demonstrations. "And in case of doubt, one should not abandon the sacred scriptures so interpreted by the Holy Fathers," he wrote. As justification for his and the Church's position, he closed his letter with a quote from King Solomon: "The sun rises and sets, and returns to its place."

Such antiquated reasoning from someone as respected as Bellarmine caused Galileo's gorge to rise. He announced to his friends that it had become necessary to travel to Rome to properly defend his position face-to-face with the men who figured largely in this affair. Serious attempts to disabuse him of this plan were made by Galileo's friends: Federico Cesi stressed that he not try to vindicate himself against Caccini and urged him to keep his peace about Copernicus. Cesi cautioned him that

Bellarmine automatically smelled heresy wherever a scientific theory appeared to contradict scripture.

Galileo's longtime friend Maffeo Barberini, who had been a Cardinal since 1606 and the bishop of Spoleto since 1608, urged him not to venture beyond physics and mathematics. He wanted Galileo to grant theologians their territory, thereby denying an opening to his enemies. Barberini, an astute politician as well, added that Galileo's enemies would distort anything he said.

"If you say the moon has mountains, they will quote you as saying the moon has people on it," Barberini suggested.

Giovanni Ciampoli, Galileo's former student from the University of Pisa who had since joined the ducal court in Florence as well as influential circles in the Roman Curia, stressed that Galileo had many friends and a few noisy enemies who, by their words and actions, made themselves out to be quite numerous. Ciampoli told his friend to relax.

But Galileo couldn't. He was fired up and chomping at the bit to extract justice from the world for the suppression of what he believed to be true. And to his friends, he sang the same song: he would attempt to justify his scientific position without invalidating anything in the Bible.

As he wrote in one widely circulated tract, "I hold the sun to be situated motionless in the center of the revolution of the celestial orbs while the Earth rotates on its axis and revolves about the sun. They know also I support this position not only by refuting the arguments of Ptolemy and Aristotle—especially some pertaining to physical effects whose causes perhaps cannot be determined in any other way, and other astronomical discoveries. These discoveries clearly confute the Ptolemaic system, and they agree admirably with this other position and confirm it."

In his mind, the phenomena to which he referred had been

already conclusively demonstrated. But for the prelates who had been immersed in Church dogma for most of their lives, these new phenomena were far from demonstrable. Ironically, Galileo was still considered a potential threat, especially to those who believed his ideas.

Chapter Twenty-Four

When Galileo departed for Rome in December of 1615, he caused a lot of unwelcome noise in the Holy City. But, undaunted by the challenge of storming the Holy City with truth, Galileo successfully enlisted Cosimo's help in furthering his cause.

Cosimo sent instructions to his subjects in Florence and the Holy City to make Galileo's stay at the Florentine ambassador's Medici palace as comfortable as possible. Ambassador Guicciardini was anything but pleased at the prospect of Galileo's arrival, and wrote to Cosimo's secretary:

Cardinal Bellarmine himself warned me that should Galileo overstay his welcome here, the Inquisitors will be forced to weigh in on a conclusion about his tidings from the moon. Please tell the duke that I am uncertain as to whether Bellarmine has changed his mind or his attitude, but I do know that some Dominicans prominent in the Holy Office and others think ill of him. This is not a place to come to dispute about the moon or, at this time, to bring new ideas.

Galileo is not a patient man and will not hearken to any

advices. He is fired up over his opinions, and has a passion about them that he lacks the strength and prudence to curb.

But Cosimo's support remained unflagging. He testified about Galileo to a relative at the Vatican, writing, "I know him well. He is a good man and very observant and zealous in religion." Cosimo also wrote to Cardinal del Monte requesting that he introduce Galileo to "intelligent and discreet people" who would welcome his "correct and pious intentions."

Galileo's presence at the ambassador's palace sparked numerous conversations between him and curious Roman cardinals and opinion leaders. Gradually, they learned of Galileo's earnest religious feelings, which secured and increased his honorable reputation at the Vatican. By the beginning of 1616, Galileo felt bolstered that the groundwork for his onslaught had been firmly laid.

Amidst all the activity with Galileo, Pope Paul V secretly directed Cardinal Bellarmine to assemble a panel of eleven consultor theologians. They were to investigate the proposition that the sun was the center of the universe.

But the Church had long been protected by a pack of dogmatic Aristotelians who simply handed the pope what he wanted: justification for continuing the Church's narrow-minded assumptions about the cosmos. After deliberating for five days, the panel's unanimous conclusion was a predictable parroting of what it had been ordered to declare. The notion that the sun was the center of the universe was "absurd in philosophy and formally heretical," and the idea that the Earth actually moved was the same and also "at least erroneous in theology."

This came as not exactly a list of charges, but a warning that the acknowledged hero of the telescope was treading on thin ice. A warning was as far as Bellarmine and Pope Paul were willing to go. Galileo's Copernican theories would be relegated to interesting hypotheses meant for salon discussions and academic debates. They would never be considered valid by the Church.

By late February 1616, word had reached Pope Paul V that Galileo was still noisily promulgating Copernicanism in Rome. Thus, Paul ordered Cardinal Bellarmine to formally caution Galileo to keep his discussions within purely hypothetical confines. This was meant as a mild first shot across Galileo's bow, coming indirectly from the pope himself. Or so they thought.

At the same time, the Holy Office suspended Copernicus's decades-old book as heretical, unless and until someone corrected it, because Copernicus was no longer living. The Holy Office supposed that Galileo, still alive, might not be intimidated.

Summoned to meet Bellarmine, Galileo went to him feeling heartened that he had done his duty as a scientist by telling all who would listen that his own eyes had not deceived him, nor had his calculations. History was on his side.

As he thought of what Bellarmine would say, Galileo prepared to defend himself. He would use the tool of rational discourse to eviscerate popular arguments against Copernicanism. At the same time, he would paint himself as a pious Catholic whose sole interest was to safeguard the Church from setting its foot into an embarrassing quagmire of erroneous astronomical adjudications. Galileo had no idea that he was summoned to Bellarmine at the pope's request, nor that the outcome of the panel's deliberations had been a foregone conclusion.

Entering the anteroom of Bellarmine's house, he thought he heard the faint sounds of an argument coming from another room. Inside, Michelangelo Seghizzi was speaking with Cardinal Bellarmine. Seghizzi was the same Dominican hound who had deposed Caccini just the year before.

"Galileo has been a seed in the files of the Holy Office for some years, Your Eminence, and now his heresy has sprouted. That has been made clear in the report of the consultors," Seghizzi said. "He is too influential in too many powerful circles. He must be squashed as a heretic."

"You speak rashly, Seghizzi, but I doubt you would confirm such views in a sober moment," Bellarmine said.

"I would, Your Eminence."

"We should not rush to judgment because things are rather unclear. Everyone in Florence and Rome is on guard about a business of such importance," Bellarmine said.

Put in his place for the moment, Seghizzi tried to calm his passion to obliterate Galileo.

Galileo waited for a long time in the anteroom. His mind turned to a recent meeting with Bellarmine at his Roman office. "Signor Galileo," Bellarmine had cautioned him, "if there were a true demonstration that the sun is the center of the universe and the Earth in the third heaven, and that the sun does not circle the Earth but the Earth circles the sun, then one would have to proceed with great care in explaining the scriptures that appear contrary. One would have to say we do not understand the scriptures, not that what is demonstrated is false."

Bellarmine looked out a window as he peeled an apple, then continued. "But I will not believe there is such a demonstration until it is shown to me, nor do I think such a demonstration will ever be likely."

As Galileo mused in the present about how he could give such a demonstration, he was ushered from the anteroom into a large drawing room with a roaring fireplace and a half dozen red-robed cardinals warming themselves near it.

"Ah, you're here. Now we can get down to the business at hand," said Seghizzi, arrogantly not acknowledging Galileo by name. Galileo naturally felt slighted—knowing Seghizzi by sight and by reputation, his alarm bells went off. This was going to be no picnic.

Galileo ignored Seghizzi and nodded deferentially to Cardinal Bellarmine. "How are you, Your Eminence? You wished to see me?" Galileo asked.

Also stunned by Seghizzi's tactlessness, Bellarmine nodded back to Galileo. "Yes, Signor Galileo. We wished to notify you formally of the panel's disposition on the Copernican question."

"I appreciate the courtesy you have shown, Your Eminence." Galileo took a chair a bit too close to the fire, then moved to another.

"Too hot for you?" asked Seghizzi, taking full advantage of the double entendre with a covertly hostile smile. Galileo, by now thoroughly irked, ignored this sophisticated lout and waited for Bellarmine to speak.

"By way of preface, Signor Galileo," began Bellarmine, "we've asked you here today out of respect for your standing in your profession and your position with the Tuscan court. We are churchmen, and you are a valued scientist in immeasurable ways. As for ourselves, we have chosen our profession because we believe man cannot attain truth through science, but only through God's truth as revealed in the scriptures. We do, however, grant you the right and the freedom to pursue your scientific interests as long as they do not intrude on religious territory."

He paused, more for effect than anything, then gestured to

a scroll he was holding. "The consultors have concluded that Copernicanism does indeed tread onto religious territory. They have declared to the Holy Office that the proposition that the sun is the center of the universe is absurd in philosophy and formally heretical, and that the proposition that the Earth has an annual motion is absurd in philosophy and at least erroneous in theology.

"Additionally, Signor Galileo—and this is meant as a friendly warning—we require you to abandon your opinions on the subject. If you should not accede to this warning, a formal injunction will be issued against you to abstain completely from teaching, discussing, or defending this doctrine and opinion. If, thereafter, you do not acquiesce to the injunction, you will be held in the custody of the Holy Office and tried for heresy."

A door had been slammed shut in Galileo's face. The silence was deafening. The others stared at him, awaiting his response. Not yet sensible to the finality with which he had been confronted, Galileo readied himself again to defend Copernicanism and to find a peaceful détente between science and religion.

"I beg to reply to your Grace on this subject. I—" he began.

"Additionally, Signor Galileo," Seghizzi interrupted abruptly, "you are ordered to abandon completely the opinion that the sun stands still at the center of the universe and that the Earth moves. And henceforth you shall not hold, teach, or defend this opinion in any way whatsoever, either orally or in writing."

Galileo was stunned, and Bellarmine even more so—he had planned to drop the matter at the warning step, with no need to go further. What in God's name was Seghizzi thinking? Or was he thinking? It was clear to Bellarmine that Seghizzi had jumped the hurdle, skipping over the intermediate step of the formal injunction in response to Galileo's possible future violation of the warning. This unauthorized ejaculation from Seghizzi had never been the intent of the consultors or Bellarmine or, more importantly, Pope Paul, who overall had been positively disposed toward Galileo for some time. But the horses were out of the barn.

Unknown to Bellarmine, Seghizzi had done his undercover job well—directed not by Bellarmine nor the pope, but by a zealous senior Dominican closeted like a mole within the Holy Office. Like a dutiful hound always on guard against heresies, the man operated independently of the rest of the Holy Office. He would see to it that Seghizzi was rewarded for his treachery; indeed, four months later, Seghizzi was consecrated as Bishop of Lodi in Lombardy.

As for Bellarmine, he knew his options. He could report Seghizzi immediately to the Holy See for overstepping his bounds by altering the pope's intent and immediately remove Seghizzi from the Holy Office. Or he could choose the politically safer option: let the scene play out to see whether Galileo swallowed the hook so artfully inserted by Seghizzi. And if Galileo agreed to be hamstrung by such an arbitrary, unsanctioned edict, then so much the better—even though Copernicanism was seen by the Vatican as a relatively harmless hypothesis. Indeed, the only ones seriously threatened by the theory were sundry academicians and other members of the Pigeon League whose careers depended on perpetuating Aristotle's and Ptolemy's flawed astronomy.

For his part, in that instant of Seghizzi's usurped authority, Galileo was too stunned to hear the din of his own confused thoughts: *Does Your Grace really demand that of me, that I be prohibited from discussing it, even hypothetically? They can't be serious. Anyway, if I choose to, I can always petition the pope to retract such a prohibition.*

Instead, a mentally castrated Galileo quietly assented. "I understand," he said.

Bellarmine would deal with Seghizzi later, but for Galileo, it was too late. He had agreed. Later, on the sly and in concert with another Dominican in the Holy Office, Seghizzi made sure to memorialize Galileo's assent in an addendum to Bellarmine's official record of the meeting, which he sneaked into the files after the fact. The sneaky rat was taking no chances.

Fortunately, a criminal usually leaves a clue behind, and in this case, it was an obvious one: Seghizzi's addendum to the record was not signed by anyone—should anyone look closely, they could speculate that it was not officially authorized by the Holy Office. It nevertheless became part of the permanent record of the admonition to Galileo within the files of the Holy Office, and was assumed to be an official part of the record of the matter.

Chapter Twenty-Five

It was left to Ambassador Guicciardini to inform Cosimo of Galileo's failed mission. He wrote to the duke, "Everyone feared his coming here would be prejudicial and dangerous." There were obvious hints of gloating and schadenfreude in his letter, but Cosimo ignored all that, loyal as he was to his brilliant friend, Galileo.

Still, Cosimo worried about Galileo's future in Rome, with a record like that. He wrote to him, asking him to use more grace and discretion in the future. A request easily complied with, thought Galileo. Moreover, Cosimo wasn't under the Holy Office's injunction—Galileo was. And if Galileo thought about it at all in retrospect, no credit was due to the duke for protecting him from the Inquisitors and the pope.

Not long after Galileo was warned by Bellarmine, the Inquisition, as per their normal routine, distributed a List of Prohibited Books to prevent Catholics from reading texts that challenged the Church's beliefs. The list outright banned Father Foscarini's contentious pamphlet. Copernicus's book on his theories too was banned, pending a posthumous edit to remove its most offending passages.

At the same time, rumors spread that the Inquisition had

tried Galileo for heresy and that he was made to abjure. To set the record straight, Galileo requested Bellarmine affirm in writing that Galileo had not been on trial, was not forced to abjure, and that he merely received a prohibition about the matter. Bellarmine promptly complied, but his letter did nothing to quiet the rumormongers once its contents were publicized. And it was those rumormongers who influenced loose cannons within the Church such as Seghizzi, who seemed to be on their own Counter-Reformation crusade against all heresies great and small.

Thus, one day in the Piazza della Rotonda, Galileo encountered yet another run-in with a triggered prelate. They were debating the effect of Galileo's discoveries within the Church and the public spheres.

"The entities of the Church and the State should remain separate for the good of man," Galileo stressed, "regardless of how arrogantly you abrogate the rights of man and how you arrogate to yourselves the rights of the State."

"But we *are* the State!" the prelate cried.

"*Monsignor*," Galileo interrupted, "do you forget that Jesus advised us to render unto Caesar the things that are Caesar's, and to render unto God the things that are God's? In that case, Caesar served as the State. You cannot be the Church *and* the State."

With righteous indignation, the churchman replied, "Oh, how glibly you proclaim your independence from us!" With that, the monsignor made his convenient getaway, leaving Galileo more than irked but less than enraged. He felt he had pushed the envelope and won. And without a word of Copernicanism, at that.

After the prelate had departed, Galileo sought a carriage

back to the ambassador's palace, where he took refuge in his pocket notebook. He wrote:

> *What fools these churchmen be when they venture into the realm of philosophy. After all, philosophy is written in this grand book—the universe—which stands continuously open to our gaze. But the book cannot be understood unless one first learns to comprehend the language and interpret the characters in which it is written. It is written in the language of mathematics and its characters are triangles, circles, and other geometrical figures, without which it is humanly impossible to understand a single word of it. Without these, one is wandering about in a dark labyrinth.*

Fortunately for Galileo, in the coming year, he had other fish to fry—aside from his duties for Cosimo, of course. And Galileo had no pressing need to promulgate Copernicanism—that was a wholly voluntary task for a knight errant, but he had not sufficient armor nor weaponry for the task of neutralizing pigeons, much less so for slaying Vatican dragons.

Already, in early 1616, he had become interested in two other issues. One involved determining longitude at sea by means of eclipses of Jupiter's satellites, which would be a potential source of income from governments and their navies. And later, Galileo began to study comets too—after three had appeared within a two-month period, he was flooded with notes from his colleagues and fans, including Archduke Leopold of Austria, requesting his theories on them.

While they fascinated him, Galileo knew neither of these

studies would remain unresolved for long. He also knew that the heightened public and scientific interest in them would eventually wane. Nevertheless, he waded into the debate on their significance, knowing he could mask his views under the names of his former students, and that they were an opportunity to steer clear of anything even vaguely Copernican.

Ultimately, Galileo wanted to catch up on research for two books he had promised Cosimo before he arrived at court in Florence. So, in March 1616, after Galileo had long been silent about the sun and the Earth, he found himself in an audience with Pope Paul V as a result of his February appeal to the pontiff regarding accusations of heresy coming from reactionary Counter-Reformationists in the Church who had read the treatises he had written before Bellarmine's warning. These tracts were circulating widely across Europe and were stirring up a hornets' next of angry resentment. His earlier ideas, now suppressed by the Inquisition, were coming back to haunt him. Even his friends were earnestly imploring him to steer clear of the subject of Copernicanism. They didn't want to lose him to the dungeons of the Inquisition, or worse, to the stake. As for Paul V, he had waited some weeks for the Counter-Reformation furor over Galileo to die down before granting him an audience.

Walking and talking together in a garden near the papal apartments, the first words from Paul were an assurance that neither he nor the Holy Office would listen to slanders and that Galileo could feel safe as long as he lived.

"Thank you, Your Holiness," Galileo said, "but I am under an admonition from the Holy Office not to discuss the relationship between the sun and the Earth."

"I know," Paul said. "I'm the one who ordered it, though

not exactly as it turned out, thanks to that Dominican hound, Seghizzi."

Ah, so it was Seghizzi, after all! thought Galileo. *No wonder Bellarmine looked so stunned.*

Paul seemed to read Galileo's mind. "Ultimately," Paul added, "the most charitable view to take of the matter is that Seghizzi simply misunderstood the admonition I had suggested, and in his zeal enlarged upon it—something our mutual friend Cardinal Barberini greatly regrets, as do some others in the College of Cardinals."

After the damage had been done, that was a bitter pill for Galileo to swallow, but he replied diplomatically. "I understand, Your Holiness," he said.

"Galileo, you must put this whole matter aside in favor of your *real* scientific pursuits. Are there no new discoveries on your mind these days, such as the moons of Jupiter?" Paul asked.

Galileo knew he was getting somewhere. He might be able to get at the ultimate scientific reality via a back door.

"Why, yes, Your Holiness," Galileo said. "There are other books I want to write—about how things move in the world; how they are stopped; what makes them change course while on a trajectory; what factors form their trajectories, and how one celestial body in the spheres may affect another without touching it directly. These ideas have been of great interest to me for some years."

Paul yawned. This was all over his head. "Well, if you concentrate on those studies, you have no fear of attack from any quarter as long as you live. I can guarantee that in a papal edict," he said. Though he would never follow through on it, it sounded good at the time.

"Thank you, Your Holiness. I am greatly relieved by your kind consideration."

Galileo kissed a ring on Paul's outstretched hand, and then he was off. Galileo had accomplished an abbreviated mission—not to convert the pope to Copernicanism, but to lay the foundation for future cordial relations with this or with any future pontiff. If only temporarily, Galileo had decided to present the public front of an amenable disposition and had just gotten a perceived reward for it. At this juncture, he knew to leave well enough alone, and was congratulated on this by many friends and colleagues.

Paul too was pleased Galileo had remained silent on the proscribed subject, and regretted that the overzealous Seghizzi had commandeered the original purpose of the meeting between Bellarmine and Galileo. Paul prided himself that Galileo learned through him how many of his fans at the Vatican regretted what had happened at Bellarmine's house. It was all just an unpleasant misunderstanding. Of course, that was not what the official record showed. But records are best left forgotten in dusty old boxes, thought Paul.

After his meeting with Paul, some prescient instinct made Galileo reinforce his friendship with Cardinal Barberini. They began by exchanging poems, such that, by 1620, their friendship was sufficiently so well-cemented that they were on a first-name basis and had frequent conversations over wine and poetry.

Not that it greatly grieved him, but Galileo's mother died in August 1620. Barberini knew Galileo and his mother were not close. Because he had needed special dispensation from a Cardinal to get his daughters admitted to a convent, Galileo had been forced to confide in Barberini as to why: he had wanted to marry his mistress, Marina, but his mother put a stop to it, owing to Marina's lesser social position and impure past. As such, his mother knowingly blocked Galileo's goal of legitimizing his daughters by marrying Marina.

Galileo never forgave his mother for dooming his daughters to drab, poverty-stricken existences in a convent. Nevertheless, Galileo had lost a parent. So it was partly out of compassion for Galileo that Barberini, after her death, sent his friend a book of his own poetry that included "Adulatio Perniciosa" ("pernicious adulation"), a poem Barberini had written in Galileo's honor. One of its verses read:

Galileo, your skill, not always splendid, tender,
blackened in the sun,
shines forth with the glory of power.

Chapter Twenty-Six

Soon after his mother's death, Galileo found himself in a period during which he felt God was smiling on him. A series of fortuitous events came in relatively rapid succession. The following January, in 1621, Galileo was elected consul of the Accademia Fiorentina, which sought to standardize the Italian language. While this was not Galileo's bailiwick, he felt he could not afford to turn down any significant positions, honors, awards, or accolades, given the past trajectory of his career.

Then, that same month, Pope Paul V died. In February 1621, Paul was replaced by Gregory XV, whose papacy lasted only two years until his death.

But within days of Gregory ascending the papal throne, Galileo's friend and patron, Duke Cosimo II, also died. Briefly, Galileo's fate within the Florentine court was in question.

However, the continuity of his protection was ensured by the regency of Queen Christina, to whom he had written his famous letter years before. And, thanks partially to that letter, Christina was well disposed to honoring the late duke's patronage of his favorite scientist. The regency would hold until Cosimo's son Ferdinando came of age, so that none of the perks of Galileo's position at court were ever in danger of disappearing. Several years down the road, in spite of all the changes that would come to affect him, Galileo would still feel God smiling on him.

But during this period in 1621, Galileo was working hard on his next book, *The Assayer*, which introduced the scientific method to the Western world. Before *The Assayer*, the ruling thought pattern of the era was scholasticism, which deduced facts from critical thought and discourse. Innocuous as *The Assayer* was, it stirred the dogmatists who had given Galileo so much heartache, once again forcing them to change with the times. Galileo finished the manuscript in October 1622 and sent it to his publisher, the Lincean Academy in Rome. From there, it would pass through the Vatican's censors before being printed.

In the meantime, Galileo's wave of success rode on. That year, Tommaso Campanella's book *A Defense of Galileo* was printed, entreating the Dominicans to allow Galileo to pursue his research and ideas.

As a possible consequence—and not necessarily a mere coincidence—in the next year, 1623, the Roman censors were relatively speedy in approving *The Assayer* for publication. That August, Galileo's friend Cardinal Maffeo Barberini was elected pope, taking the name Urban VIII. Galileo wisely dedicated *The Assayer* to Urban VIII and sent him a copy. Of course, Barberini had the book read to him while he ate, and praised it highly. Galileo was over the moon. After the book's official publication in October 1623, Galileo was preparing for a victory lap in Rome, in which he might possibly enjoy the new pope's relaxation of the edict Galileo had been living under since 1616.

His daughter Virginia was then in her early twenties and had long since taken the veil as Sister Maria Celeste. She was over-joyed at her father's career successes, which had brought much light into her bleak, impoverished life in the convent. The stoic letters he had received from her in those years spoke of her cold and hunger, her frequent illnesses, losing all her teeth, and her overall misery in, as she described it, "this wretched world."

Nevertheless, her letters showed the joy she had in helping Galileo and the convent, where she took on more than her share of the burdens, seeking to aid sisters who were suffering even more than she was. When her sister, Livia, who had chosen Arcangela as her convent name, became severely depressed from the privations of convent life, it was Celeste who sneaked in special food and wine from their father. And it was she who, with Galileo's money, managed to procure one of the best rooms in the convent not for her, but for Arcangela.

Celeste's portfolio included convent apothecary, maker of herbal potions for various illnesses, and dispenser of medical advice—of which Galileo was a major recipient, such as the direction to expend less effort gardening, especially in cold weather, and to drink less alcohol. His rewards for acceding to her advices were homemade candied fruits of which he was especially fond, although, due to her poverty, she was forced to beg him for the fruit and sugar to make them.

For his part, Galileo brought for his daughters and the convent his garden vegetables, his orchard's wine, materials to make clothes and bedclothes, and allowances large and small. He did not live richly but managed between his salaries in the sale of his produce to keep most of the people in his life happy, if not in grand comfort. Celeste wrote him in thanks, "We are over-whelmingly committed to you, not only as daughters but as the abandoned orphans we would be if not for you. I confess myself indebted for an almost infinite multitude of blessings conferred by you." Thus, her request for small favors and gifts continued—religious relics from the holy city, cloth with which to make cuffs, or the fixing of the convent clock or a broken organ stop.

One month after his book was published, Galileo received a letter from Celeste:

Most illustrious lord father,

I cannot rest any longer without news, both for the infinite love I bear you and also for fear, lest the sudden cold—which in general disagrees so much with you—should have caused the return of your usual pains and other complaints. I therefore send the man who takes this letter purposely to hear how you are, and also when you expect to set out on your journey. I have been extremely busy at the dinner napkins so you will have them before you go, as it was for this that I have been making such haste to get them finished.

As I have no cell of my own to sleep in, Sister Diamanta kindly allows me to share hers, depriving herself of the company of her own sister for my sake. But the room is so bitterly cold that, with my head so infected, I do not know how I shall remain well unless you can help me by lending me a set of those white bed-hangings you will not want now. I will be glad to know if you can do me this service. Moreover, I beg you to be so kind as to send me that book of yours that has just been published so that I may read it, for I have a great desire to see it. These few cakes I send are some I made a few days ago, intending to give them to you when you came to bid us adieu. As your departure is not so near as we feared, I send them lest they should get dry.

Sister Arcangela is still under medical treatment and is much tried by the remedies. I am not well myself, but being so accustomed to ill health, I do not make much of it, seeing too that it is the Lord's will to send me continually some such little trial as this. I thank him for everything and pray that he will give you the highest and best felicity.

And finally, with all my heart, I greet you in the name of me and Sister Arcangela.

From San Mateo, 21 November, 1623, your most affectionate daughter,

Sister Maria Celeste Galilei.

If you have collars to whiten, you can send them.

This loyal, loving daughter of his was unwittingly playing the part of the mother he never really had, and Galileo needed that love more than he knew. From Guilia, his real mother, he had only known coldness, bitter invective, recrimination, and suspicion. In contrast, Celeste's charming and solicitous ways continually endeared her to him.

He wrote back to her the same day:

My dearest daughter, Sister Celeste,

Your selflessness on my behalf has inspired in me fits of boundless gratitude. Your love and kindness means very much to me and your cakes are delicious. I wish I could take them to Rome with me and give some to His Holiness, as I know I will meet him there. I thank you in advance for the napkins, but I ask you not to trouble yourself about my collars. I will ease your burden by having them whitened in Rome. I am enclosing a little money to help with food and your pressing necessities, and also a set of the bed-hangings to keep you warm at night. As always, I pray for your good health and the health of Sister Arcangela. Please send her my love, and also, I send you my book, The Assayer, *as you asked.*

But something still preys on my mind, dear daughter. In your infinitely kind forgiveness, you asked me never to speak of it again, but my heart continues to trouble me constantly over the suffering I have caused you and your sister. You and Sister Arcangela know all the reasons why becoming brides of Christ was not the best choice, but the only *choice, given that the alternatives were far worse and could have led us to damnation. Someday, I may, with God's grace, find forgiveness in my heart to be able to pray for the soul of my mother, now three years in her grave, who in her heartlessness caused this life of tribulation to you. But I cannot do it yet, grieved as I am about your life there. I know, because you have told me, that you love your work there, and I pray with all my heart that it will ever be so. And I pray that my creator will forgive me for every single tear that you and Arcangela have shed about the life to which I have consigned you both.*

I am, and will always remain, your loving father,

Galileo Galilei

From Bellosguardo, 24 November, 1623

After a couple guilt-ridden moans involuntarily emanated from his chest, Galileo stretched his aching bones and muscles and proceeded to his garden to tend his flowers and vegetables.

Chapter Twenty-Seven

When he finally reached Rome, Galileo he had amassed plenty of laurels to sit on, having audiences with a number of cardinals, and having no less than six audiences with the pope, who could not have been prouder of his friend. For once in his life, Galileo had achieved a full measure of happiness, intuiting that he had brought the scientific method to his modern world. Even the chronic aches and pains he suffered could not bring him down from his Mount Olympus of joy.

During his final audience with Urban VIII, they had coffee and cakes in a salon in the papal apartments. Urban put down his cup and looked admiringly at Galileo. "Galileo, we have been friends for so long that I've forgotten when we met," he said.

"I well remember that night, Your Holiness," Galileo responded. "It was in 1611 at a court dinner hosted by Grand Duke Cosimo. When Cardinal Gonzaga attacked my views on floating bodies, you defended them."

"And you never thanked me for that."

"Ah, much to my eternal regret."

"No matter," Urban said. "Consider that you have received a papal pardon for the transgression."

"Thank you, Your Holiness," Galileo said. They laughed.

"To be honest," Urban chuckled, "I didn't fully understand what I was defending, but the fact that I was defending at least the plausibility of your argument was sufficient for me to proceed. Speaking of transgressions, or lack thereof, I am told you have diligently hewed the line in the eight years since you were admonished by Cardinal Bellarmine not to discuss Copernicanism as a serious theory."

"I've kept to that promise, Your Holiness."

"Such behavior as that recommends you to us as a loyal son of the Church," Urban said. Galileo nodded. "At that time, you were told to abandon your Copernican opinions, but I wish to amend that instruction."

Galileo's heart leapt at the thought.

"Henceforth, you may feel free to discuss or write upon Copernican ideas only under the condition that you treat them as hypotheses and not as viable theory."

Galileo looked extremely relieved at this.

"I see this pleases you. Am I right?" Urban asked.

"Greatly, Your Holiness," Galileo said. "And I thank you for that."

"My decision reflects the trust I have for you, my friend."

"And not 'Adulatio perniciosa'?" Galileo asked, tongue-in-cheek, recalling the poem Urban once wrote for him.

"No, my friend," Urban said with a laugh. "As long as I remain pope, the positive memory of Copernicus is secure in our mind."

Back in Florence and enjoying his newfound soupcon of intellectual freedom, Galileo was deep in a revision of an earlier treatise that used the tides of the Mediterranean as a possible explanation of the Copernican hypothesis. In the middle of that effort, an anonymous complaint was lodged with the Inquisition that Galileo's book *The Assayer* contained the theory that extremely minute, indivisible particles were the ultimate constituents of all matter. This theory conflicted with the Church's doctrine of the Eucharist, in which bread and wine are transubstantiated into Christ's flesh and blood. In its thoroughness, the Inquisition investigated the complaint and cleared Galileo of any wrongdoing.

Later in that decade, Sister Maria Celeste was forced to frequently moderate between Galileo and his son Vincenzo's incessant demands for money. Financially strapped as he was, Galileo tried hard to provide for his son, going so far as to attempt to wring money out of Spanish authorities for his method of determining longitude at sea using the satellites of Jupiter. Galileo successfully found cash flow closer to home with his friend Pope Urban, who bestowed a yearly pension of sixty scudi on Vincenzo, but it was never enough.

Both amused and irked by his predicament, Galileo chided Vincenzo one day. "It amazes me that my offspring find ever more ingenious ways to spend money they don't have," he said.

But only when Vincenzo's wife gave birth to a boy, whom they named Galileo, was Galileo's ire assuaged. And only temporarily.

By February 1630, when Galileo again prevailed on the pope for aid for his son, the papacy's resources had been bled dry of monies and positions for Urban's numerous relatives. Thus, Urban gave only Galileo—not Vincenzo—a pension of forty scudi a year. Vincenzo used up the first year's payment without breaking a sweat, testing Galileo's patience beyond all endurance. Galileo wrote to him:

Vincenzo,

You are my only son, and you know I love you. But how can I provide a future for you, so that you can survive when I'm gone? No sooner do I rescue you from the latest financial hole into which you have fallen, then you manage to find a new one? Please, Vincenzo, try to curb your free-spending ways.

Your affectionate father,

Galileo

Two months later, Galileo finished his revised treatise on the tides, retitled *Dialogue Concerning the Two Chief World Systems.* He returned to Rome to get the censors' clearance and to have the Lincean Academy print the book. After getting conditional permission to print the book from the secretary of the Vatican. (The condition being that he still had to get the Florentine censor's approval.) Regardless, Galileo returned happily to Florence. In his blind zeal, he had no idea what he'd done.

With the coming of summer, the Italian peninsula was hit with a plague outbreak that added new restrictions to commerce and travel between various Italian cities, including Rome and Florence. God was then no longer smiling on Galileo and his Italy.

Soon, Federico Cesi, founder of the Lincean Academy and major supporter of Galileo, died, and the academy died with him. So, Galileo sought another printer—given the impassibility of the roads between Florence and Rome, and the necessity of quarantine periods at major waypoints, Galileo chose to have the book printed in Florence, but sent the preface and ending of his *Dialogue* to the secretary of the Vatican for corrections.

In the spring of 1631—via Ferdinando II in Florence, who had taken over the rule of Tuscany from his regent mother, Grand Duchess Christina, and via Ferdinando's Roman ambassador, Francesco Niccolini—Galileo succeeded in negotiating with the secretary of the Vatican to have the preface and ending of his book approved in Rome and the remainder to be approved by the Florentine censors. After this long process, the *Dialogue* was finally printed in February 1632.

By then, word had long since spread of Pope Urban's new thoughts on how Galileo was to treat Copernicanism. Thus, the Cardinal Inquisitors thought it best to step gingerly and judiciously around the subject because, only dealt with hypothetically, it had never been a threat to the Church.

Added to this mix were the Dominican Hounds, always looking to persecute a hapless victim. A certain few bad hats among them found one such victim in Galileo. The Hounds and the Pigeons were not done with him—including Father Boragio Fratelli, a Dominican priest. Not forgetting the trouble Galileo had given the order in the preceding decade, Father Fratelli, who was posted in the papal apartments as a retainer, buttonholed Pope Urban one day in a salon. He had overheard Urban's conversation with another prelate about Galileo's new book, expected to arrive that week, which was rumored to feature aristocrats debating the merits of various cosmological theories.

The conversation eventually tailed off and the cleric excused himself, leaving only Urban and Fratelli in the salon.

"Your Holiness, I'm concerned for your sake about that book you mentioned," Fratelli said. "There is a character in it named Simplicio. He is one of the aristocrats mentioned. A real idiot who could not find his nose on his face if his life depended on it."

"Sounds amusing," Urban said.

"I suppose it would be, Your Holiness, except for one aspect. Galileo puts *your* words in this cretin's mouth."

"What?!"

"Yes, Your Holiness," Fratelli said. "It's difficult for us who are innocent of guile to conceive of how devious a man like Galileo is. How he operates is a study in trickery. Obviously, he is well acquainted with your position on Copernicanism and how that whole heretical hypothesis can be upended by God's will alone, if God so chooses. We in the Order, who protect the sanctity and purity of the dogma of our Holy Mother Church, agree with you wholeheartedly that it is a useless endeavor for so-called scientists to define the whys and the wherefores of how God has created all things. And yet the trickster Galileo has taken your ideas along these lines and put them in the mouth of a simpleton."

A prelude to great anger swept across Urban's brow. "No, it can't be!" Urban cried. "He wouldn't do this to me! I must see the book for myself."

And that he did that evening, as soon as copies of the book were delivered to the Vatican. Various prelates, including several Dominicans, came to the reading. The Hounds among them listened and watched in secret glee as Urban became increasingly enraged the more Galileo's character of Simplicio was portrayed as a fool. They had never heard the pontiff swear until that night.

"That traitor!" Urban pounded the arm of his chair with his

fist. "I will see his soul damned to eternal fire for this heretical betrayal of my trust!"

Fratelli, who was present and ready for this moment, added his two cents at the risk of sending the pontiff over the edge. "Betrayal it certainly is, Your Holiness," Fratelli said. "We have searched the records in the Holy Office and, in the year 1616, Signor Galileo agreed to Cardinal Bellarmine's admonition not to discuss or write about, even hypothetically, Copernican ideas. This latest book of his clearly violates that stricture."

"1616, you say?" Urban asked. Fratelli nodded.

Unfettered, wanton spite rose up in Urban's eyes. "Well, I was not aware of this. The bastard deceived me! That settles it. Call a meeting of the Cardinal Inquisitors in my chambers tomorrow morning."

Suppressing a satisfied smile, Fratelli glided out of the room, infinitely pleased with himself. He had passed a major milestone in his mission to destroy Galileo. Thus, with their deftly managed and all too effective propaganda campaign, the Dominicans had darkened the pope's opinion of the book and of Galileo.

The scientist had made a fatal mistake in ascribing all of Pope Urban's views to the simpleton Simplicio, who, of low intelligence, could only parrot the texts of the ancients and the Holy Fathers. What a grave blunder! Galileo should have predicted its consequences.

Chapter Twenty-Eight

When Urban finally managed to get to sleep that night, Fratelli's words rang in his head: "Galileo has made you out to be an idiot, Your Holiness, by placing your words in this idiot's mouth."

Although this was nothing Galileo had ever intended, Urban swallowed this nonsense hook, line, and sinker. The Dominicans had strewn dangerous ideas in Urban's ill-breeding mind. Moreover, especially because he had recently learned of the precept Bellarmine had given Galileo not to promote Copernican theories, Urban felt the painful sting of betrayal. Having never been an emotionally mature man, this event was all it took to send Urban on the trail of revenge. From being Urban's fair-haired boy with a papal pension, Galileo suddenly felt himself not just on the outs with his chief patron (other than Ferdinando), but in seriously hot water with the Inquisition.

By the time the high summer of 1632 had rolled around, the rug had been pulled out from under Galileo. Pope Urban had prohibited further distribution of his *Dialogue*, but he didn't know why. As far as he knew, he had done nothing wrong. July and August came and went in his netherworld of mystery. In September, from his garden, Galileo watched the farmers harvesting their crops in the fields. Still nothing from Rome. Galileo languished, paralyzed into inaction by the mystery of it all. Even Celeste could not console him, although she tried.

That same September, Francesco Niccolini, the Tuscan ambassador to Rome, who still held influence with the pope due to common ties to Florentine nobility, had two interviews with Urban. Both were unpleasant. In the first, on September 4, following the grand duke's instructions, Niccolini asked, "Your Holiness, the grand duke remains greatly astonished that a book in which everything was altered, added, or removed at the will of his superiors, and which passed all other inspection, should now be prohibited from being printed."

"First of all," Urban fumed, "I respectfully advise the duke not to engage himself in this matter, because he won't get through it with honor. Second, we can lay this mess at the feet of the censors, who have created a disgraceful circus! They were tricked by Galileo, a friend I've trusted."

"Granted, Your Holiness. But might Galileo be allowed to come to Rome to explain his actions?" Niccolini asked.

"Do you think that betrayer has the right to negotiate his position with the Inquisition?" Urban asked, even more upset. "He does not! His book does great harm to religion—the worst ever conceived. He has entered into our Holy Mother Church the most perverse subject one could come across—which is why he must answer for this with the Holy Office and why his book must be sent to oblivion. That is the proper mission of the Holy Office, which has been presented with the facts in this matter and is tasked with acting on them."

Urban noticed Niccolini's downcast expression and softened with genuine respect for the man.

"Francesco," Urban said, "what you fail to understand is that the Church is attacked by the Protestants on every hand for neglecting the importance of Holy Scripture. Thus, we have been forced, in the interest of our self-defense, to harden our stance against heretics, both suspected and confirmed. Such miscreants only breed more Protestants among them. If we do not, like the Netherlanders, hold the dikes from overflowing, Protestantism will flood Europe."

"I understand, Your Holiness," Niccolini said, and withdrew amicably to lick his wounds.

Later on, his anger only slightly mitigated, Urban presided over a meeting of Cardinal Inquisitors who had by then reviewed a special commission's report on Galileo's book.

"Your Holiness," one of the Inquisitors said, "the book, as well as the records of Signor Galileo in relation to the Holy Office in 1616, have been examined and the commission's findings are in the report."

Urban nodded.

"His *Dialogue* is a clear violation," the cardinal continued, "of both Cardinal Bellarmine's proscription not to promote heretical ideas such as that the Earth revolves around the sun. The book also violates your proscription to Galileo not to treat such ideas as theories but as mere hypotheses. The book clearly presents these ideas as viable theories of explanation of the world."

"Galileo has been skirting around the edge of heresy for the past twenty years, enlightening no one and inflaming many," another cardinal added. "It's time he be brought in line."

"Or brought down," said another.

"It's apparent that Signor Galileo places no value on us as

either a friend or an adviser," Urban said. "Gentlemen, painful as it is to see the ruination of one so close to us for many years, you have full authority to proceed with your case."

One day, Galileo was visited by a messenger from the Florentine Inquisitor, who handed him a summons. He was ordered to Rome to face the Inquisitors. Galileo's reply was short and to the point:

To the Florentine Holy Office,

If Your Graces will forgive me, I will address my letter to the Holy Office in Rome. Owing to my ill health and to the difficulties of travel to Rome from Florence (necessitating quarantine periods on the way due to the Black Death), it would be much better if I could meet with the Cardinal Inquisitors in Florence. If you could accede to this request, it would be greatly appreciated.

A short time later, Urban presided over a meeting with his Inquisitors. Galileo's request was denied and it was decided that, if necessary, he be *forced* to come to Rome. In response, the Florentine Inquisitor had returned to Galileo's house and found him very sick in bed with a signed letter from three doctors, indicating that he was too sick to journey to Rome. Yet again, Urban directed a meeting of the Inquisition. They rejected Galileo's sickness as a bad faith excuse. Galileo promptly received a letter back from Rome saying that if he did not show up voluntarily, he would be arrested and brought to Rome in chains.

If Galileo had any doubts about his friendship with Pope Urban, that letter made him realize their friendship was finished.

Galileo was facing merciless inquisitors who would just as soon grind him into dust as anything else. He knew his life was in the balance and that possibly nothing could save him from the pope's wrath. It was difficult for him to confront that, in spite of the inspiring times they had shared together and the endless stream of poetry they had enjoyed, Urban extended him no mercies. Of course, it was lost on Galileo that he had not summarily been thrown into an inquisition dungeon.

Benedetto Castelli, Galileo's loyal friend, had warned him to tread diplomatically in the coming months, as whatever would be decided at this point would affect him for the rest of his life. One day, Castelli came to check on Galileo and found him working in his garden. In spite of how energetically he tended to his tomato vines, Galileo looked old, frail, and sunken into himself. It was as if his body was slowly imploding from the stress of it all. Castelli stared, thinking in vain of how he could cheer up his friend and mentor.

Galileo could feel his friend was about to speak. As if reading his mind, Galileo snapped, "Don't bother."

Chapter Twenty-Nine

Galileo left Florence for Rome on January 20, 1633. On the road, he passed villages that had been hit by the plague and was careful to stay out of them. He planned to find lodgings in Acquapendente and wait out the imposed quarantine before entering Rome. In the meantime, his daughter Sister Celeste sent him a letter:

Most illustrious and beloved Lord Father,

I have not written to you until now because I was waiting to hear word of your arrival in Rome. Having learned from this last letter of yours that you are required to spend so many days in such poor lodgings, detained in quarantine in Acquapendente because of the plague in Florence, I'm extremely distressed. Nevertheless, hearing that while you lack all internal and external consolations you still maintain your health, I console myself and give thanks to blessed God, steadfastly confident that by His grace you will return to us with peace of mind and soundness of body. I entreat you to be as cheerful as you possibly can and commend yourself to God, as He does not abandon those who put their trust in Him. Sister Arcangela and I with all our hearts and without ceasing pray our Lord constantly protect you and bless you.

From San Mateo, 5 February, 1633

On February 13, Galileo finally arrived in Rome. Due to Grand Duke Ferdinando's intercession with the pope, Galileo was granted permission to stay in Francesco Niccolini's Medici palace, but was not allowed any social contacts. Being an old friend of Galileo's, Niccolini made him as comfortable as possible, impressing on him how lucky he was to be able to stay at the palace. This gave Galileo some hope of leniency.

Niccolini even wrote as much to the secretary to Grand Duke Ferdinando that February:

His Holiness has told me that he has done Signor Galilei a singular favor by allowing him to stay in this palazzo rather than at the Holy Office, only because he is a dear employee of the grand duke and because of His Holiness's high regard for the duke. Not only that, but His Holiness could have referred the entire matter to the Holy Office straight away, but instead chose the course of having Galileo's book examined by a Commission of Inquiry . . .

This was actually a gesture on Urban's part to give Galileo time to consider his position, what was at stake, and whether or not he wanted to confess outright to violating the stricture imposed on him in 1616. Results of such commissions (often with their built-in, foregone conclusions) were usually light repercussions that redounded upon those who confessed their heresies. This could have been Galileo's salvation, if he had chosen to avail himself of it.

Galileo waited at the disposal of the Holy Office for the next three months, working on his next book, *Discourse on Two New Sciences*, and corresponding with his friends and colleagues. All the while, the avenging sword of the Inquisition was poised over his head—worse than the sword of Damocles. Finally, his daily routine at the palace was broken one day in April when he received a summons to the Holy Office. He knew this would involve interrogation.

The summons began on April 12. Galileo was confined not in a jail cell or a musty dungeon, but in a comfortable apartment at the Holy Office, not far from the Vatican. He had even been provided with his own servant. He couldn't understand the conflicted way he was being treated. On one hand, it was as if he were a member of the nobility, fed like a cardinal and given freedom to take walks in the gardens. On the other hand, he was looked upon as a prisoner whose very life was at stake, depending on how he conducted himself. There was no logic to it. But would he have preferred a cold, damp stone cell with only bread and water to sustain him? Of course not. In the end, he chalked it up to the conflicted way Pope Urban felt about him, and Galileo regretted embarrassing Urban in front of the papal court.

In mid-April, Niccolini wrote again to the secretary to Grand Duke Ferdinando about this:

Indeed, there is no precedent of anyone ever having been inter-rogated during a Holy Office trial without being detained in a prison cell, and in this regard, Galileo has profited from his prior relationship with His Holiness. Nor is there knowledge of anyone else (whether bishop, prelate, or nobleman) who, upon his arrival in Rome, has not been kept at the castle or at the same palazzo of the Inquisition, subject to all rigor and strict-ness. They even allow his servant to wait on him, to sleep there, and what is more, to come and go as he pleases, and they allow my own servants to bring food to his room and to return to the Medici palazzo morning and evening. This singular treatment can hardly be considered a persecution.

Of course, that last statement was a dangerous assumption. Galileo was, after all, under arrest, imprisoned, and possibly would be on trial for what might turn out to be a capital crime. All this in spite of the level of comfort that had been afforded him.

While Galileo was snugly situated inside Holy Office apartments in accordance with his summons, his daughter Celeste, distressed as she was as to his eventual fate, wrote him almost every day to help buoy his spirits. On top of that, an anxious series of communications went back and forth between Galileo, his friends, and highly-placed allies who were naturally concerned about the outcome. Those who garnered some knowledge of the proceedings through back channels were quick to mitigate any bad news they received about the Holy Office's proceedings before passing it on to Galileo. Questions of the day were hotly debated or discussed: *Who were the Cardinal Inquisitors on the committee who would interrogate Galileo? Which ones were friendly to him? Which ones held anti-Copernican views? How long would the interrogation process last? What was the range of penalties being contemplated? What kind of disposition should Galileo present to the interrogators? How amenable should he be to their suggestions?*

Their ultimate conclusion: the deck had been stacked against Galileo.

The sickening thing was that this vengeful pope had already made up his mind as to what would happen. The only variable that could soften the eventual blow from the Inquisition was how Galileo would present the himself to the Inquisitors.

As for Urban, who was at his most spiteful and vindictive that spring, he demanded of his Inquisitors that Galileo receive a formal sentence after a rigorous examination, followed by public abjuration and formal imprisonment.

On April 12, 1633, Galileo had eaten his breakfast more nervous than usual. After the servant cleared his plates away, a clerk of the Holy Office appeared in the doorway and beckoned Galileo to follow. It was time for his interrogation.

They walked outside. A nauseated-looking sun hung dejectedly in the meager daylight. The sky was filled with leaden clouds—the kind that threaten rain but never deliver it. Galileo's demeanor matched the spiritless landscape. The world around him mirrored the hopelessness with which he contemplated his fate at the hands of the shadowy, red-robed cardinals in their dark labyrinth, who would arrogantly judge him as if they were the Ultimate Judge.

Galileo followed the clerk down long, darkened hallways

similar to those of the Holy Office in Florence. *Maybe they're all afraid of light, like the medieval vampires who were buried with bricks in their mouths,* mused Galileo.

The clerk stopped in front of the broad oaken door to the interrogation room. Suddenly, Galileo realized, in the face of an impending doom as horrible to contemplate as the Black Death, he had mindlessly forsaken the enduring expectancy of triumph over every obstacle his friends knew to be his hallmark. He recalled his blustering, undiplomatic forays into the enemy camps of arrogant pedants over the previous decades. He had made enemies of the Aristotelians when he could have been making friends, slashing through them like Achilles surrounded by Trojan foot soldiers.

But this was no consolation as he stood before that door. "The Holy Office," he said to himself, almost out loud. The clerk looked at him questioningly, then realized even this famous scientist was fearful of what would happen to him inside. Mentally distancing himself from his predicament, Galileo smugly characterized the Inquisition as a malignant pustule on the back of the populace.

No, I must not say that, even to myself. I must make them friends and allies, even though it pains me beyond measure, he thought.

And with that, he turned the doorknob and entered the room.

Chapter Thirty

The room was arranged with a defendant's chair in the relative center, although Galileo had not been told he was charged with anything. He had just been ordered to appear. Seated at tables or desks situated around the chair were several cardinals and clerics. Among them were the presiding judge, a notary, a Dominican friar, and the chief inquisitor—another Dominican friar named Vincenzo Maculano. Before Galileo sat down, Maculano administered the oath for Galileo to tell the truth. Then they began. The other friar took notes for the transcript.

"Signor Galileo, do you know why you were ordered to Rome?" Maculano asked.

"I suppose to discuss my book," Galileo said.

Maculano handed him a copy of the *Dialogue*. "Do you mean this book, which you wrote?"

Galileo examined it. "Yes, that's the book I wrote."

"Were you ever summoned before to appear in Rome?"

"Yes, by Cardinal Bellarmine."

"What was the purpose of that summons?"

"Cardinal Bellarmine instructed me to give up my Copernican ideas," Galileo said.

"Was nothing else discussed?" Maculano asked.

"Not that I recall."

"Were you not ordered to desist from arguing on behalf of Copernicanism, writing about it, or teaching it in any way?"

"I have no recollection of that, no."

"Were you not given a specific precept not to write about, teach, defend, or discuss Copernicanism in any way?"

"I don't recall that. However, there may have been such a precept given to me. I just don't remember such a direction."

The Holy Office's indictment was then read to him:

"Whereas you, Galileo, son of the late Vincenzo Galilei, of Florence, aged seventy years, were denounced in 1615 to this Holy Office for holding as true a false doctrine taught by many, namely that the sun is immovable in the center of the universe and that the Earth moves, and also with a diurnal motion; also for having pupils whom you instructed in the same opinions; also for maintaining a correspondence on the same with some German mathematicians; also for publishing certain letters on the sunspots, in which you developed the same doctrine as true; also for answering the objections that were continually produced from the Holy Scriptures, by interpreting the said scriptures according to your own meaning; and thereupon was produced the copy of a writing, in the form of a letter professedly written by you to your former pupil in which, following the hypothesis of Copernicus, you include several propositions contrary to the true sense and authority of the Holy Scriptures; therefore, by the desire of his Holiness and the Most Eminent Lords, cardinals of this supreme and universal Inquisition, the two propositions of the stability of the sun and the motion of the Earth were qualified by the Theological Qualifiers as follows:

"One: The proposition that the sun is in the center of the world and immovable from its place is absurd, philosophically false, and formally heretical, because it is expressly contrary to Holy Scriptures.

"Two: The proposition that the Earth is not the center of the world nor immovable, but that it moves and also with a diurnal action, is also absurd, philosophically false, and theologically considered at least erroneous in faith.

"Therefore, invoking the most holy name of our Lord Jesus Christ and of His Most Glorious Mother Mary, we pronounce this our final sentence: we pronounce, judge, and declare that you, Galileo, have rendered yourself suspected by this Holy Office of heresy—that is, of having believed and held this doctrine that is false and contrary to the Holy Scriptures; also, that an opinion can be held and supported as probable after it has been declared contrary to the Holy Scripture, and consequently, that you have incurred all the censures and penalties enjoined and promulgated in the sacred canons against delinquents of this description. From which it is our pleasure that you be absolved, provided that with a sincere heart and unfeigned faith you abjure the said error and heresies, and every other error and heresy contrary to the Catholic and Apostolic Church of Rome."

Bewildered, Galileo considered what had just happened. He had been, in the same breath, both indicted and sentenced. All without a trial. *What a farce*, he thought. So ended the first day's session.

Before leaving, Maculano ordered Galileo to sign the deposition he had been given. The notary had him sign the other friar's transcription.

"You shall not leave the rooms to which you've been assigned without permission of the Holy Office," Maculano said, "nor shall you discuss what has transpired here today. Swear to all of these precepts."

Galileo did so. The clerk escorted him back toward his rooms. As he followed the clerk, his rheumatism acted up, no doubt due to the stress of the trial. The excruciating pain forced him to lean on the clerk's arm the rest of the way.

When Galileo got back to his apartments, a letter from Celeste had been left for him. He opened it excitedly, knowing he could not withstand his current tribulations without her love and kindness and concern.

But after he read her letter, Galileo's pains returned to the forefront of his mind. He lay down in bed and slept to escape them. He dreamed of a wide beach. Near the water's edge, Celeste sat on the sand. With a smile, she beckoned to him, calling, "My most illustrious and beloved Lord Father." As he walked toward her, he looked into the ocean, which stretched undisturbed toward the horizon, and saw a man waving to him from the water. The man struggled to keep his head above the soft ripples. He looked familiar. As Galileo got closer, he realized he was looking at himself just as this other Galileo sank beneath the surface. Startled, he awoke from his dream.

Some days later, Commissary Maculano wrote to Francesco Barberini, one of the Cardinal Inquisitors (and the pope's nephew, one of the beneficiaries of his nepotism): "It was decided yesterday that because Galileo's book *Dialogue* defends the heretical doctrine, he as the author is thereby suspected of holding that doctrine to be true. This justifies expediting his case. No further confessions are required of him to bring his case to trial."

On further discussion among the cardinals, they foresaw problems due to Galileo's denial that the book defended Copernicanism. "What if I were to meet privately with Galileo, outside of court, and convince him it would be easier on him if he admitted to a suspicion of heresy based only on the contents of his book?" Maculano suggested.

They agreed to his solution, so the following day, Maculano came to Galileo's rooms. He found the seventy-year-old unwell in bed, suffering from rheumatism and cursing the noxious fumes of the cave he explored in his twenties that he viewed as its cause.

Maculano was empathetic. "I regret that this visit of mine finds you confined to your bed with the usual complaint, Signor," he said.

"Never mind that, Father Vincenzo. What can I do for you?" Galileo asked.

Maculano's expression darkened. "Signor Galilei, I ask that you allow me to speak with a sort of brutal earnestness."

"Father, I would not ask for anything less."

"I come to you today," Maculano said, "in an effort to avert far worse eventualities than you might suspect are imminent. I'm afraid the Inquisitors have caught you red-handed, publishing a book that favors Copernicanism, which has been judged heretical by a committee appointed by the previous pope. Nothing you can say in the trial will change that perception of the Cardinal Inquisitors. What happens from here depends utterly on how you plead to that charge, which will start as suspicion of heresy. But if you deny the charge and defend against it, it may be changed to a worse one.

"And if that happens, I cannot vouchsafe your physical safety from the civil authorities who bend to the wishes of the

Inquisitors in all things. That could mean torture," Maculano said, pausing for effect. "Signor Galilei, believe me when I tell you, you will not survive such treatment. Or if by some grace of God you do, it will leave you debilitated and bedridden for the rest of your inevitably shortened life."

Maculano paused again, noticing Galileo looked increasingly depressed as he listened.

"Feeling your sincerity and your piety, I have searched my soul for some other solution to this ominous progression of events. I hit upon one idea, which I have already discussed with the Inquisitors and to which they assented. If you will admit to me and to the Inquisitors that you wrote the book knowing its affect beforehand—that of a positive view of Copernicanism—I think I will be able to soften the blow at the conclusion of the trial. The penalty phase of the trial will go easier on you. I pray you will see the virtue of acceding to this plan."

"Father Maculano," Galileo said with a long and hopeless sigh, "I appreciate your honest appraisal of the situation. Will you allow me some time to think of how I shall state my situation to the Inquisitors, given what you have told me? I should have a response for you by tomorrow."

With wishes that Galileo would also feel physically better on the morrow, Maculano left. When Galileo had mentally gotten some distance from this mess, he breathed a sigh of relief. His life had just been saved.

He got up to write to his daughter:

My dearest daughter, Sister Celeste,

My afflictions do pain me, I admit, but the thought of your love and concern for me is like a balm that covers over everything with its wondrous magic, yet warms me from the inside out. Yes, you have my express permission to use the funds I entrusted to you according to your best judgment and discretion. And it grieves me not a little to know that you and your sister suffer as you do in the convent.

I write to let you know that my sufferings here may soon conclude most auspiciously. One of the Church Fathers has given me a proposition today that I know will save me much grief and suffering during my examinations here before the Inquisitors. I pray that these travails will soon be at an end and I will let you know of further progress on the matter. Please use the proceeds from the broad beans from the garden for whatever you might need at the convent.

Your adoring father,

Galileo

Rome, 19 April, 1633

Laying down his pen, he finally had a moment to process the enormity of all that he was going through. With nothing left to distract him, he broke down and cried.

Chapter Thirty-One

Having feasted in the back gardens of Palazzo Barberini, a group of cardinals sat with desserts and digestives on little side tables as they listened not too attentively to musicians playing a galliard by the composer Carlo Gesualdo da Venosa. Francesco Barberini—the Cardinal Nephew, as his uncle Urban VIII liked to call him—sat at their center. He was in his mid-thirties, of slender features and wan complexion, but had intense eyes. Urban had recently appointed Barberini to the post of Grand Inquisitor of the Roman Inquisition. Not that he had any experience in that vein. He had simply benefited from the nepotism of his Uncle Maffeo, who had made him, while still in his twenties, a high-ranking career diplomat among papal legates at the Vatican. His current task, however, was to head the Inquisition's tribunal investigating Galileo for heresy.

Ironically, it was Galileo who, as a favor to the pope, had educated Barberini at the University of Pisa some years before. Now, Barberini was sitting in judgment on Galileo. Horribly conflicted as he was, Francesco was expected to show no bias regarding Galileo. As his uncle thought of it, this was Francesco's rite of passage in a ruthless and unforgiving world.

One of the other members of the tribunal, the portly

Cardinal Fabrizio Verospi, had just finished copiously wiping his face of grease and juices from the feast. He was something of a wag who, with his cutting wit, had survived several popes chiefly due to his reputation as a fine jurist. Surveying the impressive rear façade of the palace, Verospi addressed Barberini.

"*Cardinale Padrone*, I like what you've done with the refurbishments," Verospi said, mockingly using the pope's special nickname for his nephew, still jealous he had been passed over for the Grand Inquisitor job.

"*Grazie*, Verospi," Barberini said. "It's taken all of eight years to complete and yet Gian Lorenzo Bernini, better known as a sculptor than an architect, is still putting his finishing touches on it."

"Very impressive façade there," Verospi said. "But tell Bernini to fashion an abjuration pedestal for Galileo." Several cardinals laughed, but Francesco's face had a serious mien. "Why so glum, *Cardinale Padrone*? Does the impending fate of your old teacher drive you to distraction?"

Remaining serious, Barberini reluctantly answered, "You know he is a great scientist, don't you?"

"Of course. Why else would he be imprisoned in a cardinal's three-room suite at the Holy Office instead of a rat-ridden dungeon down below?" Verospi asked.

"Ridiculous," opined another cardinal.

"The old man should have stuck to science and kept his nose out of theology," said another.

Barberini defended him. "It was the Pigeon League who *forced* his nose into it by painting his ideas as heretical."

"*Cardinal Padrone*," Verospi shot back, "I'm surprised you didn't remove yourself from the tribunal, my boy. But, of course, you have your uncle's bidding to do, don't you?"

Another cardinal saved Barberini the trouble of dignifying the insult. "So do we all," he said.

Having had enough of them for one evening, Barberini stood up. "I beg your leave to excuse myself, gentlemen," he said.

"I fear, on my account, he uses the term loosely," Verospi laughed.

"Cardinal Verospi, soon the time will come when Galileo will be examined under threat of torture if he does not confess his heretical writings," Barberini said. "He's a proud, arrogant man and his pride may lead to his undoing. This is a serious business and your witticisms are not welcome."

Barberini walked off, leaving them all staring at him. A tear ran down his face—a tear of betrayal of Galileo, an old friend and teacher. How could he do to him what his uncle was asking?

Chapter Thirty-Two

The next day, Galileo met with Father Maculano and agreed to the terms he had been offered. He did not meet with the Inquisitors until April 30, when they presented him with charges:

1. That he wrote the book that had heretical ideas favored in the text
2. That he had violated the precept he had been given in 1616, and
3. That he withheld the existence of that precept from the censors in 1632.

Later, examined under threat of torture, Galileo immediately pled guilty to writing the book, explaining that his intention was never to favor Copernicanism but rather to show off his debating skills. As to the other two charges, he pled not guilty, because he did not recall ever receiving the precept. "Regarding any other charges that might arise, I throw myself on the mercy of the court." He rested his defense.

The next day, he stressed to the Inquisitors that while he admitted to knowingly writing his book to stand as in favor of

Copernican ideas, his intention was to appear erudite, with a keen scientific intellect, more than to advocate for Copernicanism. Then he misquoted Proverbs 16:18 by reminding the Inquisitors that "pride goeth before the fall." However, he relied on the documentary evidence of Cardinal Bellarmine's affidavit (that he had only been admonished to give up Copernicanism and that no such precept, as the Inquisitors had suggested, had ever been given to him), as his justification for proceeding with his book. For some reason, the Inquisitors believed him. Maybe they had gotten wind of Seghizzi's treachery years before.

On June 22, 1633, the day of the Holy Office's formal sentence, as well as Galileo's abjuration, had come. That morning over breakfast, Urban had spoken with his theological adviser, Agostino Oreggi. Urban looked glum.

"Agostino, I hope I'm doing the right thing," Urban said.

"You're doing the only thing you can, Your Holiness," Oreggi assured him. "This whole time, you have been under much more scrutiny than Galileo. You stand accused by righteous Catholics in other countries of not doing enough to defend the Church against the Protestants. We watch on the sidelines as the fate of our Holy Mother Church is decided by armies from one country fighting armies from another. We would have money to hire mercenaries but for the lucrative posts your numerous relatives have secured. And so, we watch and wait. I will be frank: in this struggle, your friend Galileo is expendable. You can't risk defending him right now."

Urban was unhappy. "As much as he's betrayed me, I'm still turning my back on an old friend."

"So be it, Your Holiness. The Lord will be his ultimate judge."

With regret, Urban turned his attention to his other pontifical duties. He thanked Oreggi for acting informally as his confessor.

The hush in the church of Santa Maria Sopra Minerva, appropriately ominous for the gravity of the situation, was barely disturbed by a few subdued voices that could not mask their underlying excitement. Most of the voices belonged to Jesuit and Dominican monks and priests who glowered at each other from either side of a wide aisle.

Among the Jesuits sat Christopher Scheiner, he of the sunspot grudge, who for years felt upstaged by Galileo. His insufferable smugness pervaded all his features, even his posture. Exulting in the glory of his victory over his nemesis, Scheiner waited with a few friends in the cavernous room of the Dominican Order's convent of the church. They had been told to expect Galileo shortly. And then, of course, the cardinals of the Holy Office would come after. There were protocols for an abjuration.

This dessert for my eyes and ears, this humiliation of Galileo, Scheiner thought, *has been years in coming.* He smiled, feeling the glow of vindication as he sat in this plush chair on the right side of history. In a hundred years, Galileo's name would be forgotten in the mists of time. But he, Scheiner, would be famous. *The discoverer of sunspots! Admittedly, I'm no Columbus, but still . . .* he thought.

A Jesuit friend sitting next to Scheiner nudged his arm and nodded toward the entrance. "Here he comes," he said.

Head bowed slightly, body covered by the white robes of a penitent, and with a slow gait, Galileo walked past rows of the seated witnesses. Scheiner's eyes lit up in perverse glee. He would have preferred to view his nemesis in sackcloth and ashes, but this would do.

"Are you ready for the coup de grâce?" his friend asked.

"As Achilles, I've been ready to slay my Hector for a long, long time," Scheiner said.

Galileo surveyed the room as he walked. Just whom, among his enemies, had been summoned by the Holy Office to gloat at his abject humiliation? Suddenly, his eyes met Scheiner's and his spine went cold. Scheiner gave him an imperious nod, feeling truly like Achilles in this moment: superior to his equals, and equal to his superiors.

Scheiner's friend noticed their exchanged glances. "Ah, Scheiner," he said. "Galileo, who is about to die, salutes you." Scheiner smiled.

As he had been instructed, Galileo stood for the sentencing. Maculano read it from a scroll along with the resulting punishment. Much of it was similar to the indictment read to him in April, the sentence and the punishment having all been decided ahead of time.

"It being the case that you, Galileo, son of the late Vincenzo Galilei, a Florentine, now aged seventy, was denounced in this Holy Office in 1615; that you held as true the false doctrine taught by many, that the sun was the center of the universe and immovable, and that the Earth moved and had also a diurnal motion; that on this same matter you held a correspondence with certain German mathematicians that the sun is the center of the universe and does not move from its place is a proposition absurd and false in philosophy and formerly heretical; being expressly contrary to Holy Writ; that the Earth is not the center of the universe nor immovable, but that it moves, even with a diurnal motion, is likewise a proposition absurd and false in philosophy, and considered in theology erroneous in faith.

"Invoking, then, the most holy name of our lord Jesus Christ, and of his most glorious Mother Mary, for this our definite sentence of Galileo Galilei, guilty, here present, confessed, and judged.

"We declare that you, the said Galileo, by the things deduced during this trial, and by you as confessed, have rendered yourself vehemently suspected of heresy by this Holy Office—and in consequence thou hast incurred all the censures and penalties of the sacred canons, and other decrees, against such offenders imposed and promulgated. From these we are content that you should be absolved, if with a sincere heart and unfeigned faith you abjure the aforementioned errors and heresies and any others contrary to the Catholic and Apostolic Roman Church, after the manner we shall require of you.

"And to the end that your grave error and transgression remain not entirely unpunished, and that you may be more cautious in the future, we order by a public edict that the book of *Dialogue* of Galileo Galilei be prohibited, and we condemn you to the prison of this Holy Office during our will and pleasure. As a salutary penance, we enjoin on you that for the space of three years you shall recite once a week the Seven Penitential Psalms, reserving to ourselves the faculty of moderating, changing, or taking from all other or part of the aforementioned pains and penalties. And thus, we declare, order, condemn, and reserve in this."

Seven of the ten cardinals in the trial signed the sentence. The other three abstained, Barberini among them.

Expressions of unqualified glee and triumph permeated the faces of Tommaso Caccini, Scheiner, and various other

Dominicans and Jesuits who had been invited to this travesty. Maculano then ordered Galileo to get down on his knees and recite his abjuration. The physical pain of getting down on his knees and the emotional pain of the shame and embarrassment of abjuring in front of a room full of people, many of them his enemies—it was too much for the old man. Somehow, Galileo found the courage he needed and wiped his tears away. For Caccini and any other Pigeons who happened to be in Rome, this was the schadenfreude event of the decade.

Trembling with suppressed rage, Galileo read from a scroll. "I, Galileo Galilei, son of the late Vincenzo Galilei of Florence, aged seventy years, tried personally by this court and kneeling before you, the most eminent and reverend Lord Cardinals, Inquisitors General throughout the Christian Republic against heretical depravity, I swear I have always believed, I believe now, and with God's help I will in the future believe all the Holy Catholic and Apostolic Church hold, preach, and teach. But because I, after having been admonished by this Holy Office to abandon the false opinion that the sun was the center of the universe and immovable, and that the Earth was not the center of the same and that it moved, and that I was neither to hold, defend, nor teach in any manner whatever the said false doctrine; and being notified that the said doctrine is contrary to Holy Writ, I did write and cause to be printed a book in which I treat of the said already condemned doctrine, and bring forward arguments of much efficacy in its favor, without arriving at any solution."

Galileo cleared his throat. Even though he knew what was coming, he glanced at the next line he was to read. He had been ordered to recite it as loudly as possible, but what he really wanted was to scream out loud at the top of his lungs, "This is insane!"

Instead, he read aloud: "I have been judged vehemently suspected of heresy—that is, of having held and believed that the sun is the center of the universe and immovable, and that the Earth is not the center of the same, and that it does move.

"Nevertheless, wishing to remove from the minds of your eminences and all faithful Christians this vehement suspicion reasonably conceived against me, I abjure with sincere heart and unfeigned faith, I curse and detest the said errors and heresies, and generally all and every error and sect contrary to the Holy Catholic Church. And I swear that in the future I will neither say nor assert in speaking or writing such things as may bring upon me similar suspicion; and if I know any heretic, or one suspected of heresy, I will denounce him to this Holy Office, or to the Inquisitor and Ordinary of the place in which I may be.

"I also swear and promise to adopt and observe entirely all the penances that have been or may be by this Holy Office imposed on me. And if I contravene any of these said promises, protests, or oaths—which, God forbid!—I will submit myself to all the pains and penalties that by the sacred canons and other decrees are against such offenders imposed and promulgated. So help me God and the Holy Gospels, which I touch with my own hands. I, Galileo Galilei, have abjured, sworn, promised, and hold myself bound as above. In token of the truth, with my own hand, I have subscribed the present schedule of my abjuration, and have recited it word by word. In Rome at the Convent of Santa Maria della Sopra Minerva, on this twenty-second day of June, 1633. I, Galileo Galilei, have abjured as above, with my own hand."

Chapter Thirty-Three

Finished with signing the document, Galileo was forced to summon all his strength to keep from collapsing on the floor, let alone rise to a standing position. Greater still than his physical pain was the venom he harbored for the seven cardinals who had signed away his freedom. Indefinite arrest! He might be under house arrest for the rest of his life, for all they cared, unfeeling lackeys of the pope as he felt they were.

Now, almost solicitous, Maculano escorted Galileo back to his apartments with a clerk of the court. When the clerk left, Maculano sat with him a while, assessing Galileo's mental state to assure himself that this persecution would not culminate with any rash acts on Galileo's part. He watched the tears run down Galileo's cheeks. The trial was over. Now, Maculano could afford to be even more compassionate with him.

"What did I do wrong, Father? How did I bring all this on myself?" Galileo cried.

"We studied your case extensively, Galileo," Maculano said. "Again, I will be brutally honest. If you had not abrasively tried to ram Copernicus down our throats, with no definite proof of his theories, and if you had not presumed to argue about scriptural meanings and interpretations of the Holy Fathers of the

Church, we would have been quite happy to leave you to your telescopes. But you forced the issue on us, and possibly used subterfuge with the censors and the pope as well. Galileo, we will not be forced."

Galileo understood. He broke down, then looked up into Maculano's eyes as a penitent would to his confessor. "Forgive me, Father, for I have sinned," he said.

"Do your penances faithfully, my son. God will forgive you. That is what's important now. The Lord will not abandon you because of what you have done. He knows you are a loyal Catholic. If nothing else, you have clearly proved that. Signor Galilei, I will pray for you to have peace in this life, as well as peace in the next."

While he was thus imprisoned, Galileo received a letter from Celeste:

Most illustrious and beloved Lord Father,

Just as suddenly and unexpectedly as word of your new torment reached me, so intensely did it pierce my soul with pain to hear the judgment that has finally been passed, denouncing your person as harshly as your book. I learned all this by importuning Signor Geri, because, not having any letters from you this week, I could not calm myself, as though I already knew all that happened.

My dearest father, now is the time to avail yourself of the prudence that the Lord God has granted you, bearing these blows with the strength of spirit that your religion, your profession, and your age require. And because you, by virtue of your vast experience, can lay claim to full cognizance of the fallacy and instability of everything in this miserable world, you must not make too much of the storms, but rather take hope that they will soon subside and transform themselves from troubles into as many satisfactions.

In saying all that, I am speaking what my own desires dictate and also what seems a promise of leniency demonstrated toward you by His Holiness, who has destined for your prison a place so delightful whereby it appears we may anticipate another com-mutation of your sentence conforming even more closely with all your and our wishes; may it please God to see things turn out that way, if it be for the best. Meanwhile, I pray you not to leave me without the consolation of your letters, giving me reports of your condition physically and especially spiritually. Though I conclude my writing here, I never cease to accompany you with my thoughts and prayers calling on His divine majesty to grant you true peace and consolation.

Sire's most affectionate daughter,

Sister M. Celeste

From San Mateo, 2 July, 1633

By the time, Galileo received Celeste's letter, he had already been offloaded from the Holy Office's apartments to house arrest at the Tuscan ambassador's palace in Rome. Ambassador Niccolini received him with all the cordiality and compassion of an old friend. Galileo had by then recovered somewhat from the shock of being seen as an outcast and had taken the longer view.

"Well, you lost the battle, eh, Galileo?" Niccolini said.

"But I won the war," Galileo replied. "All across Europe, my book is in the hands of intelligent and powerful men."

"You'd best keep such thoughts to yourself, or the pope could change his mind about you."

Indeed, in July, after he appealed to the pope on the subject, Galileo was informed that his next place of house arrest would be at the residence of his good friend Ascanio Piccolomini, archbishop of Siena. Galileo was aware that the plague still complicated travel between Rome and Florence. He wrote of this change of venue to Celeste, who confirmed the need for caution about not returning prematurely to Florence. Galileo simply moved from one palace to another, inching closer to Florence. As for the archbishop, he didn't think much of the Inquisitors' judgment, and even less of their punishment. For six months, he put up Galileo magnificently with fine wines and good food at mealtime, accompanied by musical entertainment and the stimulating conversation of great minds. Galileo, his spirits enlivened, was even inspired to continue writing his next book on mechanics.

One late summer night, Archbishop Piccolomini and his guests were enjoying a seafood extravaganza of mussels, squid, octopus, shrimp, and clams. Suddenly, a latecomer entered the hall, interrupting their dinner.

"Gentlemen, allow me to introduce my good friend Teofilo Gallaccini to you," Piccolomini said as Gallaccini and the guests began shaking hands. "He's a lecturer of logic and mathematics at the University of Siena. Gallaccini has just written a book comparing our modern architectonic principles to the mathematical principles of ancient architecture, as written in the encyclopedia of Pliny the Elder in the first century after Christ."

Having just been introduced to Galileo, Gallaccini asked, "And what do you occupy yourself with these days, Signor Galileo?"

Galileo smiled. "I occupy myself with what I can observe directly, professor," he said.

"Good answer, Galileo!" cried Piccolomini with a laugh.

Gallaccini looked a bit miffed. "And what have you observed lately, Signor?" he asked.

Aha, thought Galileo. That testy question meant his usual game with academicians was afoot. "I've recorded a number of observations in my new book, a treatise on the subject of mechanics, full of curious and useful speculations," he said.

"And the book's title?"

"*Discourses and Mathematical Demonstrations Concerning Two New Sciences.*"

"Hmm," Gallaccini sniffed.

Reminded of the days of verbal combat in the intellectual salons of Florence, Galileo moved in for the kill. "Have you ever seen the moon up close, Signor Gallaccini?"

"No. It's too far away," Gallaccini said.

"Would you care to go up to the loggia and take a look?" Galileo offered.

Minutes later, the dinner guests were grouped around one of Galileo's telescopes, taking turns marveling at a view of the moon up close.

"My word," said Gallaccini. "It looks a bit like Earth!"

"Yes, and what did the ancients have to say about that?" Galileo asked.

"Well, both Heraclides Ponticus and Aristarchus of Samos mentioned, in the third and fourth centuries before Christ—or was it the second and third centuries . . ."

"Does it matter now what they had to say about the moon *two thousand* years ago?" Galileo asked.

After the dinner festivities had died down, Galileo and the archbishop had digestives on the terrace and talked. "Your Grace," Galileo said, "I am so appreciative of your hospitality. I have almost forgotten the monstrous injustice to me in Rome."

"Don't forget, my son, that to turn the other check and to forgive is to be godly."

"I must confess, I have not been able to forgive, but I am more likely to—verbally, at least—bash the cheeks of my enemies."

"Ah, you mean all those who disagree with you?" Piccolomini asked.

"Yes," Galileo chuckled. "That has been my downfall."

"Why?" asked the archbishop.

"I can never forget what I learned from a friend in Rome who is close with the Jesuit Father Grienberger," Galileo said. "Had I known last year how to keep on good terms with the Jesuit Fathers of the Collegio Romano, I would live gloriously in this world. This father once said, 'Galileo caused his own ruin by thinking too highly of himself and despising others. Had it not been for that, none of his misfortunes would have come to pass and he would have been able to write as he wished about anything—even the motion of the Earth.' So, you see, it is not because of this or that opinion that I have been attacked, but because I am not liked by certain Dominicans and Jesuits."

"Forgive them, Galileo. Don't hold fast to your anger at them. After all, they are on the same side as you, allied with you against the devil," Piccolomini said. "Remember what Jesus said in the Book of Luke, 'Father, forgive them, for they know not what they do.'"

"It's difficult for me, Your Grace."

"Then try to forgive yourself."

"For what?" Galileo asked.

"For trying to force Copernicanism on them, and greatly angering the wrong people. I know them. They consider themselves the sole arbiters not just of biblical knowledge, but also knowledge of the Earth and the heavens."

"That's too much to chew on, Your Grace."

"You shocked them with your novelties, Galileo," Piccolomini said. "And you erred by being too arrogant and abrupt. Thus, you made enemies of them when you could have made them friends."

Forced to consider this confrontation, Galileo fell silent.

"You could never win with them, my friend," Piccolomini continued. "You stood victorious over them at the scientific level, but you could never have predicted they would shift their hostilities to the theological battlefield. There, they had you at their mercy. Believe me, I know whereof I speak. I've also worked at the Holy Office, which is conveniently close to the Collegio Romano."

Galileo sighed. Tired of conversation, and with much for Galileo to reflect on, the two of them retired inside for the night.

Chapter Thirty-Four

In December 1633, owing to the appeals of Niccolini and entreaties of the Medici family, Galileo received word from the Holy Office that he was allowed to return to his beloved villa in Arcetri, so close to Celeste's convent in Florence. Of course, he immediately sent her news of this.

Some days hence, Celeste sat writing a reply in her cramped cell. The year of Galileo's absence from Arcetri, and the intense stress of the dire danger to her father's life, had worn her down to a shred of her former self. She was pale, much thinner, constantly hungry and weak, and looked much older that the early thirties of her body's age.

When Galileo arrived at Arcetri a few days later, he wanted to kiss the Florentine earth when he had alighted from the litter. He had barely unloaded his baggage when he rushed to see Celeste. His heart had been filled with immeasurable joy at seeing her convent in the distance.

Her smile told him she had grown into a loving woman, innocent of guile and only too happy to share what she could, within the constraints of her poverty, to bring a little comfort and happiness to her father as well as others.

In her zeal to protect Galileo from the horrendous indignities from which he suffered, she did whatever she could to humble herself for his benefit. For Celeste, life was about love without preconditions, just as she felt God loved her without preconditions. Knowing this about his daughter, Galileo's guilt about having a hand in her sad fate redoubled on itself. He had finally concluded that the life she was forced to lead was his responsibility alone and not his mother's.

Galileo found Celeste in the refectory, as it was their mealtime—if it could be called that, as anything resembling a meal was pure happenstance. Each nun had been apportioned a few spoonfuls of oat porridge, a slice of dried ox meat, and a little wine. Galileo stood in the entryway. No one had noticed his arrival. They were all silent, focused on taking what sustenance they could from the meager offerings. Galileo's heart leapt when he saw Celeste sipping wine at the end of a table.

"Daughter!" he cried, words rushing from his lips almost involuntarily.

She looked up along with the abbess and the other nuns, who let out a chorus of joyful cries. Celeste ran to her father and embraced him tightly.

"Darling Celeste, how I've missed you!" Galileo said.

She kissed his cheeks and giggled like a schoolgirl at his scratchy beard. "It's wonderful to have you back!" Celeste said. "Are you hungry? We have so much to tell you! Have you stopped at your house yet?"

The other nuns crowded around them, chattering like magpies. Even the abbess weighed in. "Signor Galileo, our stomachs are half empty, but seeing you, our hearts overflow with gladness," she said.

They had seen him almost every day for years and then, suddenly, he was gone for ten months. A patron he was for these Poor Clares—and a famous one, if blemished with a little infamy: his constant gifts to his daughters were always somehow converted into charity for the convent. That, along with Galileo's frequent visits, laughing and joking with them, bringing gifts and foodstuffs, had caused him to be long and sorely missed.

But today he had returned to the fold. Lost on the sisters was the fact that he looked weakened, not much physically, but spiritually. Celeste and her friends were already thinking about the celebration they had been planning since word of his return had reached the convent. And he was home, finally! They would celebrate long into the evening hours. Galileo had brought victuals with him to share with everyone, but he saved special treats for Celeste and her sister, who, as was often the case, was unwell and confined to bed. With the abbess's permission, Galileo visited Sister Arcangela in her cell to share some delicacies he had brought. Earnestly, he got on his knees and prayed to Saint Mary for her speedy recovery.

When he and Celeste were finally alone, due to his own condition, Galileo had his first chance to take in the extent of Celeste's grave and tenuous physical state. Smiling, she lovingly took her father's hand. "You look well, father, for what you have been through," she said.

"The archbishop has treated me exceedingly well for these many months, but imprisonment it has been, and will possibly be for a long time to come. It sucks the life from me. Every day I awaken, it is as if I open my eyes to a nightmare that never ends," Galileo said. Deep sadness permeated his features. "You don't look well, Gina. Your face is so pale."

"I know, Papa. I have tried various remedies . . ."

"It seems we have *both* been broken on the wheel," Galileo said, chuckling bitterly. Celeste's lips quivered in grief, and he took both her hands in his. "But we're still here. And we're with each other."

"Yes, Papa." The light in her eyes reminded him of how, as a child, she would run inside from playing and jump into his lap to kiss him on the cheek.

"We won, Gina. We survived!"

"Yes, Papa!" she cried.

Tears streamed down his cheek. "I could not have survived it without you. You know that, don't you?" he asked.

"I love you, Papa." He pulled out his kerchief and wiped her tears from her cheeks.

"And I love you, my darling, sweet girl."

"I kept all your letters," she said, laughing softly. "They're all wrinkled and torn because I reread them whenever I'm at the end of my tether in this prison."

With his coat sleeve, Galileo wiped away his own tears and sniffled.

"I will knit you some more nose cloths," Celeste said.

He smiled, then took on a fatherly mien. "You don't eat enough," he said. "It's too cold here. You don't get the rest you need, and you are too solicitous of others' welfare to look after your own."

"I can't help it, Papa. There are many here worse off than I. Oh—I forgot to give you the accounting for the garden vegetables and the wine!"

"That can wait. Thank you for looking after everything in my absence. It's a miracle that you managed it from the convent."

"I had help. From the boy here in the convent, from Signor

Rondinelli, from people at court such as Geri who admire you and care about you . . ."

"But you were the boss of them all, directing them here and there. I stand in awe of what you've accomplished," Galileo said, beaming.

"It's you who is worthy of awe, Papa. I've read your *Assayer*. I see the virtue of what you have been telling me all my life about the fruits of observation and experimentation. What a brilliant mind you have."

Galileo smiled. Admiration from his own daughter made everything he'd been through worthwhile.

In the ensuing days, Galileo continued visiting the convent, and Celeste brought him up to date on all the ups and downs, comings and goings, and ins and outs of his household during his absence. She had kept the accounts in good order, and within a week he was happily doing a final edit on his new book, *Discourses on Two New Sciences*. In spare moments, he was back in his garden, dutifully weeding his beets and cabbages.

One of the conditions of his return was, naturally, that he not leave his house and grounds. It was true that he had been sentenced to perpetual incarceration; however, in common practice within the Holy Office, that could have meant house arrest for a term of three to eight years. But given Urban's spite and vindictiveness as a betrayed pope, it really was house arrest. Squelching Galileo added to Urban's image as a strict Counter-Reformationist. Clearly, Galileo had been in the wrong place at wrong time with his agenda and attitude. And he had paid a dear price for it.

Another condition of his house arrest at Arcetri was that he distance himself from his fans who were keen to discuss Copernican theories. As such, he was not allowed to make his venue a sounding board for these dangerous ideas. To ensure this, the Holy Office kept Galileo's house under constant surveillance. However, they couldn't keep him from seeing his daughter almost every day. Now that Galileo was home, it seemed that the years of hardship Celeste had endured had finally caught up with her.

Chapter Thirty-Five

In March 1634, Galileo learned during a visit to the convent that Celeste was ill in bed with a fever. She had contracted dysentery. If she had been in normal health, she could have survived it, but years of malnutrition coupled with exposure to cold weather had severely compromised her immune system. Her health declined drastically, day by day. Celeste fought the infection of her colon for several weeks, constantly attended to by her fellow nuns as well as her distressed father, but as March turned to April, she was thin as a rail, having lost so much fluid and body mass. It was clear to Galileo that his darling Gina did not have long to live. She received him bravely one morning, having endured severe pain during the night.

Galileo knelt by her bedside. "Daughter of mine, how are you feeling?" he asked.

"I want to leave this prison, Papa," she said, slowly and weakly. "And this wretched world. The Spring of Heaven waits for me as God's gift for the privations I've suffered in this short winter of my tortured life. I'm at the doorstep of eternal spring." Her eyes glistened with otherworldly light. "I've made my confession to my loving abbess. I'm ready to meet my Lord and maker."

Emotionally exhausted as he was from weeks of watching his daughter waste away before his eyes, Galileo could not hold back his sobs.

"Don't weep, Papa," Celeste consoled him. "You should rejoice. I'm forgiven of my sins and I will soon have my reward of everlasting life."

"Do you forgive me, Gina?" he asked. "For causing you a life of misfortune that has led to this."

"Oh, Papa. Thanks to you, I've had the good fortune to walk the path of righteousness with which the Lord has blessed me. It is you who must forgive me for leaving you so soon. With more time, I could have eased the burden of what you suffer," she said, smiling serenely. "And I could have made you candied citron in your older years."

"Darling Gina, you have already long since given me more than any daughter should have to give to her father. Thank you, my dear heart." Galileo babbled on through his tears, pouring out his heart to her. Then he looked up at her face. She had gone.

Behind him, he heard several nuns reciting a prayer in unison as some cried, "All-powerful and merciful God, we commend to you our beloved Sister Maria Celeste, Your servant. In Your mercy and love, blot out the sins she has committed through human weakness. In this world she has died; let her live with You forever. We ask this through Christ our Lord."

They covered her body, then helped Galileo up to a chair. He sat enveloped in their tender compassion, in spite of their grief.

The abbess put her hand on his shoulder. "Rejoice, my son," she said. "She is in Heaven now, with the Lord."

Galileo desperately squeezed her hand. A guttural sob of grief mixed with relief and hope escaped his lips. "I didn't do enough for her."

"No, my son. She was so happy to love you and do for you, and we are happy to love you still, as we know that you love us."

As much as the abbess comforted Galileo, Celeste's death was like a dagger in his ribs. It was not supposed to be like this, he thought. She should have far outlived him. He tortured himself that she had lived and died in a cold, damp cell—her prison cell, she had called it—while he was being wined and dined by dukes and Cardinals. Every time he thought of that appellation, pangs of guilt shot through him.

One day, Galileo sat alone, having finished his morning coffee. He started a letter to his friend Elia Diodati, a publisher in Paris:

Dear Elia,

My melancholy, my sadness, suffuses my body as water would a plant. I neglected her for so long that now Celeste calls out to me like a spirit from the beyond. If only she could have taken as good care of herself as she did for others, she would be alive and hugging me with her arms tightly around my shoulders. I can't bear the grief.

The intense pain of losing his favorite child had barely lessened. To distract himself, Galileo hunched over a scroll he had written over thirty years before—to no avail. A single sob escaped his throat. He had failed her. If he had had more money back then, he never would have put his two daughters in a convent. *I could have borrowed money for dowries from friends! I could have done something!* he thought.

Wracked with guilt, he prayed, "Can you forgive me, Jesus? I beg you to forgive me. She never had the life I wished for her.

She never lay in her husband's arms at night. She never cooed at her newborn son. Knowing she was unworthy for marriage, she lived only to help me, and what did I do for her? A little money once in a while?" He snorted in disgust at himself, then broke out in sobs.

A student knocked at his door. "Signor Galilei, are you all right?" a voice asked.

"Go away!" he shouted, glaring at the door.

"*Sì, sì!* Excuse me!" The student's muffled footsteps faded away in the distance.

He returned to his letter to Diodati, summarizing his plight:

I trust you are well. I have lost my daughter Celeste, not to the plague, which she feared, but to a much simpler ailment she could have survived, had she not been so weakened by years of privation in the convent. The grief of this follows me day after day and week after week. I fear I will never get over losing her. I must summon all my strength to work on the book you have asked for. I thank you for your willingness to distribute it in France when it's ready. I'm also working on another book, which reviews and summarizes my early experiments with an inclined plane in order to demonstrate the laws of motion. I will tell you when that one is ready also, but it will take time. I'm old now and I struggle to understand what I saw so clearly many years ago. Give me time.

As for myself, I am confined to this little villa a mile from Florence with the strictest prohibition against going there and against having meetings with many friends together. So I live quietly, frequently visiting the nearby convent where Celeste resided, a woman of fine mind and singular goodness and most affectionate to me. And returning home, just the day before she died, a deputy of the Inquisitor came to tell me of an order from the Holy Office in Rome that I stop asking for permission to return to Florence or they will make me return to a real prison of the Inquisition. From this and other incidents, you see that the wrath of my most powerful persecutors is continually aggravated. But whenever the stupidity of these small-minded men enrages me, I fall back on this dictum: they can ban me from most human discourse, they can ban my Dialogue, *but they can't ban my ideas.*

With great affection, from my prison in Arcetri,

Galileo Galilei

26 October, 1634

Chapter Thirty-Six

Tears ran down Galileo's cheeks. He sealed his letter to Diodati and picked up another document. It was Celeste's birth record and a horoscope he had written for her on the occasion of her birth. He read it aloud to himself: "'21 August, 1600, daughter of Marina Gamba of Venice, born of fornication the thirteenth of this month and baptized by me, Giovanni Viola.'"

He thought to himself, *Born of fornication, not marriage. And henceforth unsuitable for marriage, and having a father who had no dowry. What else could I do but give her to the convent?*

He looked again at the paper. *I loved her, but not as much as she loved me*, he thought. *I wasn't fair to her. She gave me so much.*

He looked again at the horoscope and continued reading to himself. "'A certain discord between the rational and sensitive powers of the soul is indicated. Because Mercury is very powerful and in a ruling sign, whereas the moon is weak and in an obedient sign, her reason will be ruled by emotions. Saturn, which indicates a person's morals, foretells that her character will be upright and serious, though tinged with some venom. This, however, is softened by Jupiter's beneficent and powerful square aspect with Mercury. This makes her solitary and taciturn, but capable of enduring hardship and troubles. However, Libra, a human sign, vouches for her gentle conduct toward others and her tranquility.

"'Also, the fortunate sun grants some personal authority and loftiness of character. As for her intelligence, Mercury, who is endowed with much authority, promises a creative intelligence. And because he is associated with Jupiter, this increases her wisdom, prudence, and gentleness. An auspicious and powerful Saturn especially helps her memory. Libra, ascending with many planets, also favors intelligence. Spica rising further contributes charm and reverence for God.'"

Sadly, he said aloud, "No wonder she never protested."

It took Galileo months to arrive at some kind of rapprochement with his guilt about Celeste and Arcangela. Celeste had appealed to him before she died, pleading with him to help Arcangela and the convent as best he could. He was fulfilling that promise by visiting Arcangela regularly and taking more of an interest in her and the convent's affairs.

When Galileo had finally put together the manuscript for his *Mechanics*, he contacted a Venetian friend to help get the book approved for publication by the Venetian Inquisitor. He was promptly refused outright: Rome would not allow Galileo to publish *anything*, Copernican or not. Thus, thanks in part to Urban VIII's spite, the Inquisition had made itself irrelevant to modern man. To Galileo's advantage, however, its omnipotence was decentralized beyond the Italian peninsula, which gave him the ability to publish abroad.

Around that time, Galileo learned secondhand that *The Assayer* had lit the fires of a scientific renaissance in Europe. All across the continent, wherever scientists gathered or worked, scholasticism was slowly being replaced by the scientific method of experimentation, observation, and deductive thought processes. In the trial of Galileo, a few bad hats in the Church had won the battle over men's minds, but they were clearly losing the war.

Galileo's triumphs in the publishing world—most of his books were translated in German, French, and Dutch—rapidly made their presence known across Europe beyond the Inquisition's jurisdiction. Even his *Letter to the Grand Duchess Christina* was published in Latin and outside of the papal states, in Italian. Encouraged by his friends to keep writing and publishing, Galileo had become not a national treasure, but a pan-European treasure. His observed truths were crossing national boundaries at a mad rate.

Coincidentally, just as he decided that he had accomplished all he could astronomically, an ophthalmic disease took the sight from first his left eye, and then his right. Although it pained him greatly to lose this sense, he had the advantage of old age, which affords a larger, more dispassionate view. And in this case, it didn't matter—others had already picked up the mantle of his research efforts. Astronomers around Europe had begun searching for ways to demonstrate the truth of the Copernican ideas he had championed for years. Meanwhile, the progressive calcification of the Inquisition was never more in evidence than in its intractability regarding the Galileo case.

Chapter Thirty-Seven

In this period of physical decline, though still in possession of his intellectual acuity, Galileo received a visit from the English epitome of modern man, John Milton. Long since an accomplished man of letters, Milton was only thirty-one when he visited Galileo in Arcetri as part of his European tour. He had no trouble communicating with Galileo, as he was fluent in numerous languages, including Italian.

One day as they sat on Galileo's back patio, a new assistant named Vincenzo Viviani served them coffee. As he poured cups for them, he held back from asking a pressing astronomical question of Galileo. Already showing promise of becoming a brilliant mathematician and scientist, Viviani sighed in frustration and returned to the kitchen for some cheese and fruit.

"Signor Galileo," Milton said, "it's clear to me, as well as many others who have read your books, that you are a force who looks uncompromisingly at nature and who says what he knows to be true."

"Thank you, but it doesn't matter what I've said," Galileo said. "What matters is what I've written."

"And for that, I very much regret the tremendous suffering you must be undergoing, given the iron fist of the Roman

Inquisition." Galileo shrugged. "This gross encroachment against the freedom to think and speak our minds is something that lies entirely outside the bounds of civilized society. It must stop if we are to enjoy the liberties of free men."

"Tell that to the pope," Galileo scoffed. "He'll either take that to heart or report you to his Holy Office."

"And then the Holy Office can most ceremoniously stuff it, Signor," Milton replied.

Galileo laughed so hard that he cried, releasing decades' worth of pent-up emotions.

"I have nothing but compassion for what you have endured, Signor," Milton continued. "I have witnessed firsthand in France and Spain what atrocious acts this most unholy of holy offices has committed, and I bemoan that this tyranny of thought has also reached Italy."

Galileo nodded, dabbing his eyes with a handkerchief.

"What kept up your spirits during your infamous trial by those small-minded bigots who are far from your equal in intellect or honor?" Milton asked.

"My wonderful daughter Gina, who, five years since, left this world for the Holy Palace of Heaven."

"I'm so sorry."

"But she didn't keep my spirits up; she gave me her own spirit. So much so, that when I was finally home after almost a year's absence, she must have felt her mission on Earth was over."

"The love of a daughter, wife, or mother can take the heights of Heaven not one bit further," Milton said, nodding.

"It is as you say, English bard." Galileo said. Milton laughed, then turned to him in earnest.

"What, Signor Galileo, has driven your astronomical discoveries?"

"The warmth of a hot meal and a good woman," he said, laughing. "To be honest, that's what I think about on the roof on cold nights, looking at the stars. A hot meal! But, I suppose I've always been a curious sort, never satisfied with the simple, accepted answers for things, such as, 'The Milky Way is impossible to understand with only the naked eye to view it. I was always asking 'Why?' and 'Why not?' to such barriers to knowledge. I say, 'To hell with barriers to knowledge!'"

"Here, here, good friend!" Milton cheered. "As our poet laureate, William Shakespeare, once wrote, 'Ignorance is the curse of God; knowledge is the wing wherewith we fly to Heaven.'"

"I have heard of this great poet. What else has he written?" Galileo asked.

"'A fool thinks himself to be wise, but a wise man knows himself to be a fool.'"

"Wonderful! A very wise man. Signor Milton, you are circumnavigating Europe on your tour. What is your goal?"

"Knowledge," Milton said with a smile. Galileo laughed, then got up to escort Milton into his dining room for lunch.

As they sat down at the table, Galileo elaborated, "Knowledge. A few truths from the infinite and eternal mysteries, that's what I've been after."

"To what end?" Milton asked.

"Knowledge brings us closer to God."

"That's too profound for lunch."

"Then we'll save that for dinner," Galileo said.

The next morning, Milton stood on Galileo's front stoop before taking his leave.

"Signor Galileo, I have enjoyed your hospitality, your *buona cucina Italiana*, and most of all, your friendship and conversation." He pulled two books from his satchel, including a bound copy of his latest poem, *Lycidas*. "Please accept this as a token of my gratitude."

"*Molto grazie*, Signor John!" Galileo held the book close to his chest, nodding in appreciation.

"And you, sir," Milton said, looking at Viviani, "by the intelligent questions with which you continually pepper your master, shall also blaze across the sky like a comet one day, inspiring us with your works." He handed him a copy of *Lycidas*. Viviani was overjoyed.

"Speaking of books," Milton said to Galileo, "it does my heart good to know yours are all over Europe, even England. Those barbarians in Rome can keep you in this house, but they can't erase your name."

"And they can't erase my freedom," Galileo said.

They hugged, then Milton stepped into his carriage and was off. Galileo lifted his face to the summer sun. His beets and cabbages called out to him and he smiled. Sightless as he was, he had found a way to remove the weeds.

Epilogue

In the late Florentine spring of 1739, Giovanni sat in the café near the Ponte Vecchio. Across the piazza was Cioci's butcher shop. Giovanni's eyes never left the shop's entrance for long. As if he were the pope's nuncio sent on a holy mission to recover the Ark of the Covenant from the clutches of the infidels, Giovanni was glued to his café chair, his attention alternating between the shop and his pastoral idylls, which he slowly sketched in his small notebook.

Suddenly, he noticed a skinny boy of ten or eleven carrying a bundle of paper toward Cioci's. Giovanni erupted out of his chair like a jet of rocks and lava from the mouth of Vesuvius. Without paying the café waiter, he skirted across the piazza to head the boy off from his errand. Watching Giovanni, the waiter briefly worried about losing his tip—that is, until he saw Giovanni pay the boy, unceremoniously snatch the bundle, and head back to the café with the boy in tow.

The two of them sat down while Giovanni plied the boy with mascarpone and pastry. The boy ate as if it were his last meal while Giovanni untied the bundle of papers and discovered reams of Galileo's notes and letters. Ebullient triumph shot through him. His body glowed with a serene joy as if he had been touched by an angel. Giovanni, of course, knew that Galileo's family members, horribly shamed by his Inquisition trial, had destroyed all of his papers that they could find, fearing retribution from the Inquisition if they were discovered to be hoarding anything pertaining to the causes of his arrest and incarceration. Such was the power of the Church and its Dominican Hounds.

But Giovanni also knew the Hounds had since been sufficiently defanged, such that he could collect Galileo's papers with impunity.

After the boy had downed the treats, it wasn't hard to get the papers' source out of him. A palazzo in the Via Sant'Antonino. Something about that street jarred Giovanni's memory—but for the moment, that was all. Later, Giovanni followed the boy, whose name was Mauro Panzanini. They passed the church of Santa Maria Novella and entered the Via Sant'Antonino.

Inside, they ran into another young boy, a neighbor of Mauro's. "*Eh, Panzanini!* What do you say?"he asked Mauro.

Mauro ignored the boy's curious stare at the well-dressed Giovanni and kept walking. Mauro was on an important errand and didn't have to pay attention to the neighbor kids. He was bringing home a real gentlemen who might help his struggling family.

When they came to Number 11, Giovanni looked up at an impressive four-story urban palazzo of the 1600s. There, high above the front door, was an impressive bust of a man who looked familiar. Mauro saw him staring. "It's Galileo Galilei, the famous—"

"Ah!" Giovanni gasped, stunned.

"Two years ago, they re-buried my grand-uncle Vincenzo with him," Mauro said, looking up at the bust.

But Giovanni wasn't really listening. He was caught up in

childhood memories suddenly flooding back to him. "I used to play in this house! I was even younger than you when my father built it!" he said.

"Your father built it for my grand-uncle?"

"*Sì!* Vincenzo Viviani, the mathematician," Giovanni said. "I remember now. When he was young, Viviani was taught by Galileo himself. He used to pick me up in the terrazza inside, throw me over his shoulder, and feed me grapes and mozzarella."

Giovanni laughed at the memory, then stepped back to view the inscriptions on the plastered-over boards affixed to the building on either side of the bust. Each board was inscribed laboriously and minutely in Latin about Galileo's accomplishments. "My God! It's Palazzo Viviani!"

"No, it's Palazzo dei Cartelloni," Mauro corrected. Della Cartelloni ("of the boards") referred to what had been affixed to the front of the building in honor of Galileo.

Now, Giovanni remembered that Viviani's palazzo passed to his nephew, the abbot Paolo Panzanini; when Panzanini died, the property and all its contents came into the possession of Panzanini's nephews.

Awed, Giovanni crossed himself, feeling that God had brought him to this house for a reason. Giovanni wiped a tear from one eye and looked down at Mauro. "Could I go inside and meet your parents?" he asked.

"My mother is home," Mauro said, opening the door. In the foyer, he called, "Mamma, mamma! There's someone important to see you."

Giovanni noticed the foyer was devoid of furniture. There were marks on the walls where paintings had hung. A scrawny-looking cat walked slowly across the foyer and disappeared into another room. What was wrong with this picture? They had stripped the house bare. *Why,* he thought, *they have no money! Ergo, the sales of Galileo's letters for wrapping paper! My God, this is horrible.*

From behind him, Giovanni heard a woman's weak voice. "*Ciao, Signor.* I'm Angela Panzanini," she said.

"Mamma! He's buying the paper we have in the corn crib!" said Mauro.

More memories were coming back to Giovanni. When Viviani had died years ago, he had bequeathed his vast library of books to the hospital of St. Mary.

But the palazzo, as well as his collection of manuscripts, had gone to his nephew, Abbot Panzanini, who eventually passed on and left everything to his own nephews, Paolo and Andrea Panzanini. Giovanni turned to look at Angela, who was undoubtedly married to either Paolo or Andrea. She was the sort of woman who was thin but wouldn't have been, if she were not undernourished. Giovanni realized how hard a life this family was leading.

"*Buonasera, Signora Panzanini.* My name is Giovanni Battista Nelli," he said, voice cracking.

"What can we do for you?" Angela asked.

"Well, the circumstances under which I come to be here are . . . uncanny." He paused, looking at the empty foyer. "Is there somewhere we could sit and talk?"

It had been so long since the family had entertained a guest, Angela hardly knew what to do. She tried to mask her embarrassment. "Certainly, if you don't mind sitting with me in the kitchen. This house is so cold most of the year."

Mother Mary and all the saints, Giovanni thought. *They lack even coal to heat the house.* Aloud, he said, "Yes, of course. No need to stand on ceremony with me."

In the middle of this grand palazzo, Giovanni and Angela sat in old, sturdy chairs at an even older but venerable table in an otherwise bare kitchen. In the hearth, a single pot hung above dying embers. Angela stared at the floor glumly. Mauro listened to them from the doorway as he played with the cat. It meowed weakly and hungrily.

"We have been selling whatever we can," Angela said, "but things are getting worse since my husband lost his job at the silk factory. He would be here to welcome you, but he's looking for work every day."

"I can see how difficult this is for you, Signora," Giovanni said, sensing the grief underneath her visible frustration. "Have you thought of renting rooms, or selling the palazzo and getting less expensive lodging?"

"Viviani's will forbids it. To honor his teacher and friend Galileo, he forced his descendants to own and occupy the building. So we starve," Angela said, chuckling bitterly. "But we control it. And when the hyenas come looking to buy our palazzo, what they offer won't feed a plow horse. But we can't sell the house anyway." She shrugged and looked up at Giovanni. "When you came to our door holding the paper you bought from Mauro, it was truly God's blessing on us. I've been praying every day for Santa Maria to help us. And she listened."

Giovanni hesitated. He didn't want to appear to be stooping, out of patronizing noblesse oblige. "Maybe . . . maybe I could help too," he said. "Do you have more of that paper?"

Angela seemed too distracted by her worries to even process the question. "Oh, yes . . . I think there's a box of it somewhere. We hold on to everything we can until the last possible time. The paper you bought today will be tomorrow's polenta and wheat."

Something wrenched Giovanni's heart. In his entire life, he

had never been so intimately close to someone's poverty. It was hard to confront. After a moment, he asked, "You mentioned a box?"

Shortly, Angela held a lit candle as she led Giovanni up several flights of stairs to a small garret that long ago had been a maid's bedroom. Mauro followed at a discreet distance. Giovanni's arrival was the most exciting thing to happen to him in a long time. He hung on every word Giovanni spoke and was already extrapolating endless possibilities for his family's sustenance.

Dust covered everything in the tiny garret. Added almost as an afterthought, a tiny window shed a bit of light on the scene. The former maid's bed was covered with unsaleable junk and broken furniture. In a corner of the musty room was an old corn chest about five feet wide, four feet high, and close to three feet deep. In its day, it would have held quite a bit of corn, but it hadn't been full in a long time. Anticipating what might lie inside, Giovanni couldn't take his eyes off it.

"Is that where the paper is?" Angela said to Mauro.

"*Sì*, Mamma. There's a lot of it." Mauro looked at the bundle of paper Giovanni held. He was happy that the paper seemed so valuable to Giovanni. Mauro's family had been struggling for so long, he couldn't remember when he last had a good, full meal. Was their struggle at an end? Mauro's eyes darted excitedly between Giovanni and the old chest.

"Can I look inside?" Giovanni asked.

Angela nodded, and Giovanni nimbly navigated his way toward the chest, past miscellaneous unwanted objects scattered on the floorboards and stuffed in sacks and boxes. In spite of his efforts, he tripped on an old broom handle that instantly rolled under his foot's pressure. Angela gasped in fright. Giovanni almost fell, but righted himself. After another few steps, he stood above the chest.

Giovanni looked at Angela as if for a final approval. She smiled and nodded. The lid's hinges creaked loudly as he pulled it up. But there wasn't enough light in the room to see the contents. He motioned to Angela for the candle. With intense excitement, he held it above the chest and saw that it was packed to the brim with stacks of paper.

Giovanni riffled through a stack. There was handwriting on every page! The same handwriting as that of the mortadella wrappings. It was surely Galileo's! What a treasure, he thought. Giovanni started to speak but his voice cracked. "I can use this," he said, clearing his throat. Angela beamed excitedly. A few feet behind them, at the edge of the candlelight, Mauro grinned. "Could I ask how much would you would want for this?"

"The whole chest?" Angela asked.

"Yes. I could have movers come by tomorrow for it, if you'd like."

Angela's lower lip trembled. She thought of the years of poor nutrition her Mauro had suffered. She thought of her beloved Paolo, who was too proud to beg for food and too honest to steal it. Her gnawing stomach brought her back to the present. Giovanni wanted to know how much. She looked away from him.

"Oh, let's see . . . I don't know," she said.

Giovanni realized she had no idea what to ask for. He felt around in a coat pocket for a few silver scudi—enough to buy a family's food for a few months. He held out the coins to her. "Would this be enough?"

Angela's eyes lit up instantly. Even in the dim light, the

shiny silver coins glinted and welcomed her grasp. Mauro saw the coins from across the room and smiled proudly. His extrapolations were coming true.

Angela was speechless. "Oh, Signor!" she sobbed. "You are truly a gift from God!" She crossed herself and wiped her eyes with the sleeve of her dress.

"I'm only offering what any decent man would do," Giovanni said.

"We don't know any decent men," Angela said. "Except one." They smiled at one another.

Giovanni hired a coach to take him and his bundle of paper back to Villa dell'Ombrellino, his estate on Bellosguardo Hill overlooking Florence. This was the same Florentine suburb where Galileo once had a house over a hundred years earlier. In the fading light, Giovanni ate dinner on his terrace overlooking the beautiful gardens at the back of his property. There was such peace here. Even the birds must have gone to sleep. It was inspiration enough for his idylls. He wouldn't like to move from this place. It was on the outskirts of the city, away from all the noise, and Via Sant'Antonino was in the middle of the hustle and bustle, neighbor children yelling to one another in the street below. He supposed he could get used to it. After all, if he had found the corn chest, who knew what other treasures still languished forgotten in the obscure corners, closets, cupboards, and hidden compartments of that house? Treasures that might have escaped the Galileo family confessor's examination for objectionable material to be burned. This much was well known about the aftermath of Galileo's death: all those connected with him, by birth or otherwise, save a few who still had their integrity intact, went to great pains to ensure their safety from the Inquisitors by destroying whatever they could find of Galileo's "dangerous writings"—lest they be accused of hoarding heretical documents.

Sitting on his terrace, Giovanni cut the cords that held the bundle of Galileo papers together. He turned the handwritten pages over until he scanned a page full of emotionally vivid adjectives. This was not Galileo's hand; it was Vincenzo Viviani's. He leaned back in his chair and read from the top of the page. He knew enough already about Viviani's history as Galileo's pupil and assistant to realize that, from the sequential dates and the disarmingly personal entries, he was reading Viviani's diary, which he must have included as a sort of biographical record of his time with Galileo. What a find! What a treasure! He knew scholars who would give a finger or some teeth for such a thing.

As Giovanni read excitedly, the words echoed in his mind:

I have spent the better part of the day and night in vain attempts at raising Galileo's spirits. He completed his will yesterday and had it notarized. He knows his time is coming. Ah, my Lord and Savior, is there no hope for this Earth? This is a time when a man, if he has lived his life with honor and decency, should be able to take comfort that he will rest in the arms of our Lord. But today we received the news from Father Paolo that the maestro's remains will not be honored with a burial on the Church grounds in Arcetri. To be treated as one who has been excommunicated is the final, humiliating crucifixion for this man who has labored all his life only to give knowledge to mankind and who only desires to die in peace with men and with God.

I rebel most intensely toward this injustice perpetrated on one so undeserving of it. A knife might just as well have stabbed me through the ribs for the pain I feel for my friend. What shall I do? Shall I lie to the maestro that I have supplicated before our local abbot to have him reconsider this inhumane ruling? I must. I will entreat the abbot to have mercy on Galileo's soul. He is not a heretic. He made a mistake, but this should not bar him from entering Heaven. Please! They must bury him in consecrated ground, or I shall be wracked with guilt the rest of my days on Earth for not preventing this injustice.

Giovanni, a tear rolling down his cheek, read the next day's entry:

Galileo worsens. It is as if the news of yesterday has sapped the life from him. He asked me this morning, 'How long must I stay in purgatory because of this shame?' I didn't know what to say and my emotions got the better of me. I broke down and took hold of his hand. The great spirit that he is, he comforted me like a saint. There's only one thing I can do to spare him this agony of the worst kind. I shall make my confession afterward about it and shall say as many Hail Marys for this sin as my father confessor dictates. I saw the abbot today, very early, before the maestro had even risen. Father Guilio refused my plea abruptly and wouldn't even listen to me. He must be so afraid of angering the Church Fathers that he will not grant the slightest accommodation to this great man.

Now, while smiling to my master, I must pretend to go out of the house to supplicate the abbot. And when I come back, I must wear a happy smile and lie to my greatest friend that he shall be buried at the Church with due ceremony.

I must lie again that the abbot, who is mindful of the maestro's contributions to world science, now considers him as part of the blessed fold of the Church, and agrees with me that he should not suffer in purgatory and should be allowed to enter Heaven unhindered by what transpired eleven years ago. And I must lie again so that my first lie is not discovered: I must tell the maestro that Father Guilio instructs him to keep silent about where he will be buried, lest news of this transgression of the rules reach Rome. God forgive me that I do this. I do this for love and respect of my master, not for any personal gain, and I shall make whatever sacrifice is needed to make up for what I do today. May God have mercy on my soul and on the soul of my master.

Giovanni's mind and heart were riveted to the pages as he read them. The next entry was two days hence:

The maestro is barely alive. His is the face of death today. All the doctor and I can hear is a faint wheezing coming from his chest. He neither drinks nor eats and only waits to go. The agony I feel as I watch this unfold is only softened by the smile I saw this morning when I spoke to him. He thinks he will be buried at the Church and has provided more alms for the Church than he originally intended, so grateful is he that Father Guilio has consented as I've told him. Lord, please forgive me for what I have done. He must surely go to purgatory, but what torture for him it would be, in his final hours, to be aware of it. What pain to his immortal soul! Surely, God will bless him at last, and let him enter into the kingdom.

At that point, the handwriting changed visibly on the page, becoming stilted and sloppy, as if the hand that had put it on the page had been shaking. The ink was smudged and blurred in places, as if Vincenzo's tears had fallen upon it. Giovanni could barely make out the words:

My greatest friend in all the world is gone forever. He succumbed late this afternoon as the cook was preparing supper, which she knew would only be eaten by myself and not by the maestro. I can't bear to be in this house without him. Without his forceful nature beckoning me to do this or that, without his strong grip on my arm as I lift him from the bed, without that irreverent demeanor that has afforded me so much laughter in these darkest days of his life on Earth.

I can't bear to be inside and I cannot stomach leaving the house without him shuffling weakly on his crutches by my side. I don't want to be on this Earth either now. I want to shout at the devil and his minions in the fires below, and I want to cry out to Heaven that Galileo has suffered enough these past eleven years for his mistakes. I plead with our Lord, with our Mother Mary, and with all the saints, to remember Galileo's heart, which has never strayed one braccia from the light of the Church. I know Pope Urban has never forgiven him, but I pray with all my heart and soul that it will be different with the heavenly host. I can't go on now. That is all I can write.

Giovanni sat silently, feeling the full weight of what he had just read. He was certain no one had ever read it before.

He was not good for any useful work the rest of the night. His sleep was fitful. Staunch Catholic that he was, he himself had become worried about the fate of Galileo's soul.

By the next morning, as he breakfasted, Giovanni's thoughts

returned to Viviani's house. Still, even to contemplate buying the house, Giovanni would need his lawyer to break the last testament of the late abbot Panzanini, pleading the abject poverty of Viviani's descendants. Anything could be done if one had the will to do it. His father had told him that once.

By the time his servant came to remove his breakfast plates, Giovanni had decided. He would take his mission seriously—to preserve Galileo's legacy. And Palazzo Cartelloni was part of it.

In the ensuing weeks, Giovanni engaged an attorney, who successfully challenged Panzanini's will in the Florentine courts. Giovanni promptly gave Angela and Paolo a fair price for the palazzo, found them reasonable quarters nearby, and sold his own house on Bellosguardo Hill. Using connections within his literary society, he also saw to it that Paolo found work. Giovanni spent his leisure time exploring his new home and finding even more hidden Galileo treasures. When they were selling everything that wasn't nailed down, the descendants had not looked carefully enough. Boxes of books were secreted in hidden vestibules, originals of Galileo's physics and mathematics papers were stuffed inside built-in banquettes, and voluminous correspondences with philosophers and scientists of the last century lay scattered at the bottom of damaged armoires and side tables rejected by the furniture buyer.

Giovanni even found Galileo's prized Lincean Academy ring in a forgotten sewing box in the same garret that had held the famous corn chest. Folded up at the bottom of the sewing box was a scientific tract of some kind with mathematical calculations scribbled all over it. It was clearly not Galileo's handwriting—possibly Viviani's, but it was certainly a neater hand. At the bottom of one page, something in Galileo's hand had been passionately scrawled in large, bold script: "*Nota bene*, you puffed-up theologians. Someday, you may be forced to declare a man guilty of heresy who believes as you do now that the Earth does not move."

Many years later, Giovanni lay dying of pneumonia in his Palazzo della Cartelloni. Glancing at him momentarily, a grieving relative noticed a smile break out on his face. Giovanni Battista Nelli's *Life of Galileo* had just been published, and he was finally comprehending that he had accomplished his mission. Giovanni coughed for a few moments, sighed, then considered the book, a new copy of which lay next to him on the bed. The volume would spark many more from other authors. Giovanni chuckled weakly as he realized: the book might never have been written if he hadn't been looking for a good mortadella.

Acknowledgments

I am indebted for the opportunity to write this novel to Robert Barbera, founder of the Mentoris Project. He is a true light-bringer and so is his publishing company. Barbera is all about not just the passing on of knowledge but also the passing on of inspiration and wisdom. To that end, he has charged us writers with the mission of inspiring readers with examples of men and women—mentors, if you will—who were themselves bringers of light to the cultures in which they lived. For singular insights into Galileo the man, as well as Galileo the astronomer and scientist, I am greatly indebted to such brilliant scholars of Galileiana as John Heilbron, Annibale Fantoli, Vincenzo Viviani, Giovanni Battista Nelli, Maurice Finocchiaro, John Elliot Drinkwater Bethune, Mario Biagioli, Stillman Drake, Ernan McMullin, Dava Sobel, and Thomas Mayer, as well as to an invaluable forum for colloquies on such subjects as Galileo: the Center for Medieval and Renaissance Studies at the University of California at Los Angeles.

Peter David Myers,
Los Angeles, winter 2019

About the Author

Peter has sold, written for hire, or optioned ten theatrical feature scripts, and has done a number of rewrites for indie film and TV producers. Two short films, a stage play, and numerous TV public service announcements have been produced from his scripts.

His produced projects include nine *Chapters in Black American History*, the drama/comedy *The Pickup*, his half-hour suspense drama, *Double Cross*, as well as *Speak to the World*, a pilot for an interview show.

One of Peter's comedy feature scripts won an Honorable Mention at the Thunderbird International Film Festival Script Competition.

Peter has judged scripts for UCLA's Master of Fine Arts Screenwriting Showcase and has been a regular panelist at the West Coast Writers Conference. His advice to screenwriters is part of Tarcher/Penguin's anthology, *NOW WRITE! Screenwriting: Exercises by Today's Best Screenwriters, Teachers and Consultants*.

This is Peter's second novel. His first, *Leonardo's Secret: A Novel Based on the Life of Leonardo da Vinci*, was published in 2018.

God's Messenger
A Novel Based on the Life of Mother Frances X. Cabrini
by Nicole Gregory

Grace Notes
A Novel Based on the Life of Henry Mancini
by Stacia Raymond

Harvesting the American Dream
A Novel Based on the Life of Ernest Gallo
by Karen Richardson

Humble Servant of Truth
A Novel Based on the Life of Thomas Aquinas
by Margaret O'Reilly

Leonardo's Secret
A Novel Based on the Life of Leonardo da Vinci
by Peter David Myers

Little by Little We Won
A Novel Based on the Life of Angela Bambace
by Peg A. Lamphier, PhD

The Making of a Prince
A Novel Based on the Life of Niccolò Machiavelli
by Maurizio Marmorstein

A Man of Action Saving Liberty
A Novel Based on the Life of Giuseppe Garibaldi
by Rosanne Welch, PhD

Marconi and His Muses
A Novel Based on the Life of Guglielmo Marconi
by Pamela Winfrey

No Person Above the Law
A Novel Based on the Life of Judge John J. Sirica
by Cynthia Cooper

Relentless Visionary: Alessandro Volta
by Michael Berick

Ride Into the Sun
A Novel Based on the Life of Scipio Africanus
by Patric Verrone

Soldier, Diplomat, Archaeologist
A Novel Based on the Bold Life of Louis Palma di Cesnola
by Peg A. Lamphier, PhD

The Soul of a Child
A Novel Based on the Life of Maria Montessori
by Kate Fuglei

What a Woman Can Do
A Novel Based on the Life of Artemisia Gentileschi
by Peg A. Lamphier, PhD

FUTURE TITLES FROM THE MENTORIS PROJECT

A Biography about Rita Levi-Montalcini
and
Novels Based on the Lives of:
Amerigo Vespucci
Andrea Doria
Antonin Scalia
Antonio Meucci
Buzzie Bavasi
Cesare Beccaria
Father Eusebio Francisco Kino
Federico Fellini
Frank Capra
Guido d'Arezzo
Harry Warren
Leonardo Fibonacci
Maria Gaetana Agnesi
Mario Andretti
Peter Rodino
Pietro Belluschi
Saint Augustine of Hippo
Saint Francis of Assisi
Vince Lombardi

For more information on these titles and
the Mentoris Project, please visit
www.mentorisproject.org